FAITHFULLY DEVOTED

RAGE RYDERS: TEMPLETON

LIBERTY PARKER

CONTENTS

FAITHFULLY DEVOTED

LIBERTY PARKER

COPYRIGHT

FAITHFULLY DEVOTED

CHARACTER BIBLE

Justice

Lizzie

Kid

Riley

Ryder

Skylar

Malibu

Kassi

Tumbler

Sadie

Travler

Kaci

Jackson

Tyler *Dust*

Riptide
Julius
Andre

DEDICATION

This is always one of the hardest parts of a book. How do you choose between all of those who have been there for you, inspired you, and stood beside you?

The thing is you can't, so I'm going to do something a little different here and dedicate this book to my two PA's. Nicole Lloyd and Sharon Renee.

Nicole: When I'm freaking out, or when someone has done or said something vicious and heart-breaking about me, you've metaphorically held my hand and gave me the best advice of my life. "Just do you, and don't worry about everyone else." When I was ready to quit, throw my hands up and give up, you talked me down, lifted me up, and made me realize that I can't be who I am if I run and hide. You are not only a fantastic PA, but you are an amazing friend with a heart of gold. Thank you for standing by me and believing in me and my books.

Sharon Renee: You jumped right in taking care of my media needs. I was asked for a newsletter, lost and not sure what road to go down. When you messaged me, it was like a life jacket in a storm of complete freak out. Throughout this, you agreed to assist Nicole and make her life a little less stressful. We've talked on the phone on several occasions and you listened to me whine and cry about the unfairness of the hurt from others' words. You've never judged, only inspired and held out a helping hand and lending a shoulder. You ladies are my rock...thank you for always being my voice of reason.

~Liberty

ACKNOWLEDGMENTS

So many people to thank, where do I even begin?

To my husband, Gregory. You've not only encouraged me, you've inspired me. You keep my things organized, my coffee habit fed and get onto me when I forget to eat when I become so enraptured in my writing. I love you to the moon and back, babe.

Kayce Kyle, my baby sister, my best friend, and my confidant. We've been through some hard times and some fun times. We've had people try to separate us, only for us to come out the other side stronger. Rumors and innuendos be damned, we are, and will always not only share blood, sorrow, pain, love, laughter and family, but you will always hold a special place in my heart and soul. I love you, sissy.

My three sons, thank you for always being my heart and the reason it beats. My life would be incomplete without you three.

To my groups, Liberty's Luscious Ladies and the Rebel Guardians Insiders, you keep my spirits lifted and always remind me of why it is I continue in this unforgiving and cut-throat industry. Your support and friendships never waiver, I am so thankful for you all.

Darlene Tallman, you have become my closest friend, I trust you with all that I am. You not only edit my books, you make them the best they can be. Without you in my life, I'd still be spending money and not getting the quality that you give me.

To my readers, thank you for giving this girl a chance. I was skeptical going in, but you keep me enthralled and enjoying these characters. Thank you for loving them all as much as I do.

To #mytribe, your strength and loyalty keep me believing in us. You never judge, waiver, or question my integrity, or loyalty. You will forever be mine. Love you all <3 forever.

Kim Richards, thank you from the bottom of my heart for always believing in me and my work and for jumping in and proofreading this. I love you so much and am honored to call you my friend.

BLURB

Lizzie

I grew up knowing I would have an arranged marriage. When my father decides that it will be to a member of the Rage Ryders Motorcycle Club to further his connections, my prayer is that we can get along.

When I meet him for the first time at the altar, I'm captivated. Tying myself to a man that I've only just met seems like something out of a book, but here I am.

Justice

The club has been everything to me since I first joined out of high school. I'll do anything my President asks, but when he tells me I need to marry someone sight unseen, I question my blinding loyalty for the first time.

Until I see her. Something about her calls to me, despite my screwed-up past. Despite the man I am now as a member of the Rage Ryders.

She is mine.

Lizzie and Justice start out as a marriage of convenience, one that will help the Rage Ryders and also Lizzie's father. Can Lizzie rise above her past? Will Justice keep her at a distance because of how he grew up? It's time to ride again with the Rage Ryders and see if they'll become faithfully devoted.

PROLOGUE

Lizzie

MY NAME IS ELIZABETH DAWN CARDOZO. TODAY, I TURN thirteen years old. Instead of having a birthday party like most kids my age do, I am attending my oldest sister's wedding. There are three of us girls in total, unfortunately for my sister, it is a marriage not of her choosing, but an arranged marriage, where my father is the only one with a hand in picking her husband. Her husband to be is older than her by at least twenty years, if I had to guess. She's only nineteen years old, her husband is nice to me. He always brings me chocolate treats when he comes to see my father.

Well, he brings me, and my other sister, Rosa, chocolates, but always brings Genny flowers. Never the same kind, they're always different, but always smell so sweet. Genny is kind and respectful to her future husband, even though you can tell she's sad about marrying him. His name is Georgio Maldonado, he's in my dad's organization, but he's not mean and cold-hearted like Father is. He's always gentle when dealing with us girls. I think he'll be good to Genny, I just don't want to see her unhappy for the rest of her life.

I hope she can end up falling madly in love with him, I want to see her smile—a real smile, not the fake one she's been wearing since the announcement was made of her impending marriage.

Rosa is my middle sister, Father says she's next to be married and it has her nervous. Rosa is only seventeen years old, but Father says he's already found her a suitable husband, and he is anxious to get his life started with her. Momma isn't excited and has begged Father to wait until Rosa is of legal age. He says it's out of his hands and has promised her to him. This makes me worried about my future, I'm only thirteen, but it won't be long until I'm of age where he thinks it's acceptable for me to be married off also.

I've never had a chance to be just a kid. Unfortunately, kids in this house are to be seen but not heard. We've grown up around men who are rude and lethal, even at my age I know what they do isn't nice or even legal.

We've started learning about the law in school, which has confirmed my suspicions of my father's livelihood of not being what it should be. Father is a mean man, when we don't do what he wants, he has no problems raising his hands to us in anger or locking us in the basement for days if he wishes. I like it when school months are here, I don't get locked in the basement during the week, only on weekends. It happens more than I'd like for it to, I have a problem controlling my tongue and always speak what is on my mind.

It is unacceptable to Father, women are only good for being a good wife and mother. We are groomed from birth to be the best, so we can basically be 'sold' into arranged marriages. We are to make our father proud at all times.

"Lizzie, we need you in your sister's room, it's time for you to get ready, child." My mother calls for me. I can hear in her voice that she is sad for my sister, so I will try to be extra good today. I want this day to be as special as possible for her, so I need to mind my P's and Q's. For Genny, for Momma, and so I don't embarrass Father and pay for it later on. I'm always messing up, but today I make a vow that I will be seen, and not heard. I hate that term Father uses when he scolds us. Who can keep their mouth shut when they see something wrong, or know that they are right? I don't know that I'll ever be good at it.

"Coming, Momma."

"I know this is your birthday, child, but let's make this important day for your sister about her, and not about you getting a year older," she scolds me then promises me, "I'll make it up to you tomorrow and take you shopping…. alright?"

"Yes, Momma." I answer like the perfect porcelain doll.

"That's my good girl," she tells me with a smile on her face, it looks forced which worries me, is she concerned for my sister? Or is she just sad to see her leaving the house and starting her life with Georgio?

"Everything alright, Momma?"

"Everything is perfect Lizzie, let's go get you ready."

"Yes, Momma." My sister's wedding day was perfect, and she was so beautiful. We had a good day, and an even better time. I saw my sister smile which made the uneasiness I felt falter.

The next year we repeat the process with Rosa, she marries a man who is my Father's enforcer, he's a mean man, but seems to be fond of Rosa like Georgio does

Genny. He isn't nice to me like Georgio is though. His name is Roman Saltzer, and he firmly believes as does my father, that I should keep quiet and out of the way. Maybe he'll change his tune once he has kids of his own. One can always hope anyways.

Justice

I HIDE IN MY CLOSET WHEN I HEAR MY DAD SCREAMING AT my mom. It's the same thing every night, Dad comes home drunk, and finds something wrong that Mom's done. It could be his dinner being cold, to the laundry not folded right, to the house not being cleaned to his liking. The thing he doesn't understand is that if he came home on time, dinner would be warm, and that helping with laundry and cleaning the house is my chore to help Mom out. Mom takes the blame for it all trying to save me from his wrath. I can't wait until I'm big enough to stand up for myself and Mom. She doesn't deserve the back of his hand or the fist that often flies.

I hate hiding like a coward, but at fourteen years old I'm still not strong enough to stand up to him. Mom insists that when he gets like this that I make myself scarce and hide somewhere. My closet seems to make me feel safe even though I know he can easily get to me here. I never seem to make it on his radar, either that or he's just too lazy to seek me out himself. If I'm in plain sight I'm not safe from his anger. I've gotten a good beating from him on several occasions.

I'd rather it be me than Mom, but she says it's her job to protect me from him when he's like this, and I'm to do as I'm told and not disobey her. It's been hard to sit back and not run to her rescue, but he's so much stronger than I am. I can't wait for the day that it all changes and the roles are reversed and he's the one who's scared of me.

I hate him so much, and one day I will make him pay for doing the things he does to her, her screams are in my nightmares along with the way she always looks the next day. The only good thing about my dad is he's a good provider, he holds down a good job even though he's drunk more than he is sober.

He must be good at his job for others to turn their heads. He never leaves the house drunk to go to work, but he is always hung over and never walks through the front door after a day of work without being drunk.

I hear Mom scream and I know that her safety has been compromised, why can't we be safe in our own home? I've begged her to leave many times, she won't do it, she loves him. She may be completely devoted to him, but I don't think he feels the same way about her. He tells her all the time that if she leaves he'll kill her and run off with me. I believe that's why she stays and takes the abuse she does, fear for me and the unknown.

I tell her we can make it on our own, I can get a job mowing lawns, take up a paper route and whatever else I can find that is in my age category. I don't know if she doesn't believe we could, or if she takes his threats to heart.

I fall asleep in my closet and dream of better days, times where I protect and keep my mom happy. She never worries about what monsters will come for her at night, or fear where money will come from. I'm older and take care of her and she finally smiles all the time instead of only when it's the two of us...alone.

My dreams this night bring a smile to my face, and I know when I wake the next morning that I must make that dream a reality. If I could only figure out a way to make *him* leave for good.

ONE

JUSTICE

Joining the Rage Ryders out of high school was the best decision I've ever made. I tried to get Mom to leave Dad, but she was insistent that she was fine where she was. I don't know if she's just learned to accept the abuse, or if she truly worships him. It makes me sick to this day to think about, which is exactly why I didn't ever want an Ol' lady. What if his genes were more prominent in me than I ever knew? I never want to put someone through that the way he put her through it.

I would enjoy nothing more than to purge him from this earth, but I know I'd be the first suspect since I've been so vocal about his abuse to anyone who was willing to listen. I learned the hard way that cops aren't always on your side, they believe a parent before a troubled kid on any occasion. No matter how many black eyes were shown, or how many broken bones were set, we were pushed aside, and our word was never enough.

When an arranged marriage was brought up in our meeting, and me being the only single officer left, I nearly shit my pants. Literally. Knowing the demons that may lay within me makes me sick to think of what her life could be like with me. I've seen how it can tear someone up when they walk on egg shells just to please or not anger the other. "Fuck that shit, that's not how I want to live my life," I mutter under my breath. "We don't even know if we'll like each other, let alone be able to make a lifelong commitment to each other."

I need to talk to Ghost about this shit running through my head, he's my best friend and the only one I've confided in about my past and childhood. If I can only pry him and Bristol apart for a few minutes, I may get my talk I'm in need of. They aren't at the clubhouse, so I send him a quick text asking if I can stop by. He answers only seconds later letting me know that it is good for me to swing on by. I go to my room, grab my keys and head that way.

As I am riding and enjoying the freedom of the open road, I can't help but to think that I have three days until I say I do to someone I've never met. Yes, I'm counting down the days…I'm calling it the countdown to dooms day. The day some poor woman will tie herself to me forever. I can't help but feel a little sorry for her. I don't think her father knew what he was signing his daughter up for when he decided it was acceptable to give her to me, I don't see how I can ever make this work.

This is a business arrangement, but I don't want her to feel like she is stuck with me in all ways if that isn't something she chooses for herself. We'll have a lot to talk about on our wedding night, that's for damn sure, I need to know where she sees us, where she wants our relationship to go. Do we move forward with each other, or do we keep it business only?

I don't want to feel trapped and I don't want her feeling that way either. Fuck, this is a lot of pressure for one person to carry on their shoulders. I pull up to Ghost and Bristol's place and park my bike next to his, I barely make it to the door before it's swung open and Bristol is in my arms. They had a rough road getting to where they are today, but they survived and are stronger now than anyone could hope for, me included. She's become such a close friend of mine, that making this sacrifice for her seems worth it at times, when I'm not lost in my head that is.

"Woah, what's all this, how are you doing, sweet girl?"

"I'm good, Justice, Ghost told me what you're doing for

us, and I wish there was another way," she says with tears in her eyes as she looks up at me.

"No crying, sweet girl, it will all work out." All the while I'm thinking that I hope it does.

"I'm not crying, there's something in my eye," she says trying to make me believe it. About then, Ghost comes out on the front porch to join us.

"Hey man, how're you doing? Sweet cheeks, what happened, why are you crying?" he asks Bristol. She huffs and puffs for a second before she answers him.

"I'm not crying damnit!" she stomps her foot and heads inside. Ghost and I look at each other and start laughing. Her temper tantrums are so adorable you can't help but crack up, which eases some of the tension I've been carrying around for the past hour or so.

"What brings ya by, brother? Not that you're not welcomed here anytime you want."

"I have so much runnin' through my mind, I just can't seem to shut it up and was hoping that you'd be willin' to lend an ear."

"Always brother, anytime you need me I'm there. Let's head inside and sit in my office and talk this shit out."

"Sounds good to me…thank you."

We head inside and make our way into Ghost's at-home office. Bristol brings us some beers and we thank her before she leaves us to ourselves.

"Tell me what's on your mind," Ghost starts us off.

"I can't get it out of my head that I'm gonna end up being like my old man. It just won't go away and it's there on repeat, the memories, the failure and the shame."

"You're not your old man, Justice, and you never failed, and the shame isn't yours to carry. That burden lays at your dad's feet, man, not yours."

"I know that's the logical way to see this, but it's what's been ingrained in me so long in here," I say pounding my fist to my chest, "and in here," I say pointing at my temple on my forehead.

"That's not necessarily true though, is it, Justice?"

"What's that supposed to mean?"

"What I mean is, that if it was ingrained in you, to be abusive towards women, you would've already shown your colors with all the Ol' ladies in the club. With all of their smart mouths and attitudes I've never once witnessed you lose your cool with them. You take every-thing they do and say in stride. You're respectful to them at all times, otherwise they wouldn't trust you or care for you the way they do. Think about it, you've become one of Bristol's closest friends and confidant. She tells you things she's never told anyone else, including me, and out of everyone, she'd spot an abusive asshole before anyone else coming their way."

"That's different, they're not mine!"

"They may not share a bed with you, but they're yours all the same and you know it."

We talk it out a few more minutes before I decide I need to think on our conversation. I leave feeling better about the situation than I have in a long time. Needing to feel the wind in my hair and the road beneath my feet I head out for a long ride. It's nights like this that I feel closest to who I want to be, who I strive to be, just me and the open road.

Lizzie

MOM DECIDED TO TAKE US GIRLS TO PARIS FOR ONE LAST women's shopping week before my pending nuptials happen. Genny and Rosa are accompanying us on our trip. Their husbands were good with them being gone for a week. They're both pregnant, but not far enough along that their doctors are worried about them traveling.

This is Genny's second baby, and Rosa's first. Giovanni is my nephew and he is such a daddy's boy that we know he'll be fine with his momma gone for a quick trip. Our goal is to find me a wedding dress fit for a queen, the only problem is that I don't think we'll find biker chick wedding attire in the city of love, but I suppose you never know.

I'm mostly looking forward to spending some time with Momma and my sisters, I don't know how much time we'll all get once I'm married outside of the family. My sisters are at the house all the time because their husbands are in business with my father, but my new biker husband-to-be isn't involved, and from what I over-heard doesn't care much for my father and his business, or associates.

I'm happy about that on one hand, but on the other I will miss my family like crazy. We all still get together weekly for dinner, dressed to the nines like normal. I can't see bringing my biker groom to a dress up dinner with them, he'd stick out like a sore thumb causing my father to possibly have a heart attack.

Oh, but it sure would be fun to see the look on my father's face throughout dinner. We took the family jet to make it to Paris, so we were able to stretch out and enjoy the long journey. Once we arrived a town car showed up to escort us to the classiest hotel. We're in a huge suite with four attached bedrooms, each with their own bathrooms. There's a living quarters, and an office and that's all the exploring any of us did before we found our own bedrooms and called it an early evening.

Twelve hours later, I'm up and alert and ready to see the sights that are so different from those of home, the great state of Texas, US of A. I've always enjoyed travelling and hope those days aren't behind me just yet. Who knows, maybe he'll enjoy sightseeing and taking some adventures with me. He may not enjoy the fancier joints, but maybe we can still take in some of the great sights afforded to us.

I don't know if he has anything in mind for a honeymoon or not, but I wouldn't mind taking a road trip and getting to know each other for a few weeks. My thoughts are everywhere as we head down to the restaurant in the hotel and have a nice breakfast. Once we step out disappointment hits, its pouring down rain outside. I shouldn't be surprised, this must be an omen to this up and coming wedding. I groan out loud causing my sisters and mom to laugh at me.

"Not funny guys," I convey to them.

"It's Paris, sweetie, not even the rain can ruin this for us, now let's go on the hunt for a wedding gown," Mom says to me and we hail down a cab. We visit four boutiques before I find the dress that I feel will be perfect. It is perfect! It has a V swoop neckline which is trimmed in antique looking beads, it's short sleeved and falls just below my knees which show off my legs nicely. It's not traditional length which I find irresistible and will fit the Texas weather nicely. It's white in color which is fitting seeing as I am a virgin. You have to be in our family with the watchful eyes that follow us around, making sure we keep our purity for our future husbands.

I was never permitted to speak to boys growing up, I went to an all-girls school, so I didn't even have the opportunity during my hours away from my bodyguards. The only men or boys I've ever know belong to Father's business associate's kids, but we were never left alone so I've never even kissed the opposite sex. When I was fifteen and reading romance novels I used to dream of the day I'd get my first kiss and how someone else's lips would feel on my own.

My life has been censored in so many ways that I'm thankful that Rosa would sneak me her books after she'd finish reading them, it was our small rebellion from Father. Mother would buy them and give them to Rosa since we weren't permitted televisions in our rooms, and we were told what we could and couldn't watch when we went into the family room.

My life has been so sheltered that I'm not sure how I'll fit into the biker world. I fear I'll make a fool of myself once I get a taste of freedom.

TWO

JUSTICE

I HAVE TO SAY I'M IMPRESSED WITH HOW THE WOMEN transformed the backyard of the clubhouse for today's events. Then it hits me in the chest and I have a hard time breathing all of a sudden.

Today is my wedding day.

The day I meet my bride for the first time at the altar. The day I tie myself to a stranger, a woman I've never even met.

I do this for my club.

I do this for my brother.

I do this for her.

She deserves to be out of that house of horrors she's

grown up in. I'm standing here waiting for her with Ghost by my side. I decided on only one groomsman, and since this is to ensure his future, I can't think of anyone else that should be by my side.

I look up and see the most stunningly beautiful woman I've ever seen in my life. She's tanned, dark hair—so dark it's nearly black in color. I can't see her eyes clearly from the end of the aisle, but from here they look to be hazel in color. The one thing that's standing out to me right now is that she looks about as happy as I do to be here and meeting your future for the first time at the end of a makeshift wedding altar. I didn't want to get married in a church, therefore we set it up in the backyard of the clubhouse. It's nothing fancy, but the ladies did a good job making it something special for her.

I hope and pray that she's at least not putting me in the same category as her father. I suddenly want to prove to her that I am a good man.

I'll be good for her.

To her.

This I vow to her and myself, I will not be my father. My breath leaves my body as she heads towards me. Damn, all of a sudden, I feel this primal instinct take over and the word mine goes through my head over and over again. I've never felt this way towards another human being let alone a woman.

Lizzie

I CAN'T BELIEVE I'M ACTUALLY GOING THROUGH WITH this! I hate my father more at this moment in time than I ever have in my entire life. Why does he get to pick who we spend the rest of our lives with? As I stand with him at the Rage Ryders' clubhouse door leading into the backyard, I have the sudden thought to flee. Could I make it out of here, or would of one of father's men catch me?

Looking over at Father I can tell that if I pull one of my shenanigans today I will pay the price. A price I never want to pay again at his hands and cruelty. I decide to give fate a chance, there must be a reason this is happening to me...right?

Once the wedding march begins, I watch as my sisters start their walk where they will be waiting on me once I make it to my destination. When my turn comes, I feel the butterflies start to fly in my stomach. Please don't let him be some dirty, disgusting old man who doesn't believe in maintaining himself. Even I'm not that good of an actress, for Christ's sake! I can't help but picture a greasy, long-haired, long-bearded toothless asshole waiting to make me his. I can't help but shiver at those thoughts.

Once we get to where I can see my future husband I am shocked and pleased with what I see. He very much does take care of himself and I find myself looking forward to my wedding night. He's tall, broad and from what I see, very muscular. He's got dirty blonde hair, which isn't unacceptably long, it only reaches the top of his collar and is messy in a very sexy way. I want to run my fingers through it while he pounds into me. Holy shit, where did that random thought come from?

I make it to where he is standing waiting for me and I am suddenly mesmerized by the sky-blue eyes looking back at me. I wonder if he likes what he sees as much as I do. I work hard to take care of myself and it shows. I'm not trying to be vain, but I'm not naturally skinny so I have to work hard to where my body doesn't look bad in my clothes. I'm still no skinny minnie, but I am proud of how hard I work to make myself look presentable where he shouldn't be ashamed of me. I hope he likes all of my natural curves.

"Who gives this woman to this man?" I hear asked and turn my head to the man who asked the question. I nearly laugh out loud when I see it's another one of these motorcycle men who is officiating. I read his vest thing and it says Wasp, President. So, this is the head honcho here. He's a pretty good-looking man himself, a little older than I like, but he has kind eyes and a nice smile.

"*I* do," my father says, not *we* do, as if he's the sole reason I was born. I'm ready to get this going so I don't have to see his smug face on a daily basis. I stay facing the man performing our ceremony as he continues.

"We are gathered here today...

Justice

WE REPEAT OUR VOWS AS THEY ARE LAID FORTH BEFORE us, tying each to the other one for the rest of our lives. I'm mesmerized by her voice, it's so soothing that I can't wait to hear her talk more. I'm like a robot repeating each word after Wasp. I can't take my eyes away from hers, we're both staring into one another's and we are lost in time, it stands still until I hear those words, "you may now kiss your bride."

I lean down and kiss her lips for the first time, and there

is an explosion of emotions that hit me all at once. I start off slow, brushing my lips with hers then adding my tongue and swiping it across her bottom lip, begging for entrance. She gasps and opens up her mouth slightly, but that's all I need to insert my tongue into her mouth. I can tell she's inexperienced which drives me wild.

I grab the back of her neck and bring her closer to me, so I can get as deep and personal as possible, I want this kiss to be one she remembers for the rest of her life. She moans into my mouth making my dick stand to attention immediately. If she makes these sounds with a kiss, I can't wait to hear the sounds she'll make when I'm buried deep inside of her.

I can't wait to make her mine in all ways known to man, to feel the way her pussy clamps down on me as I thrust inside of her. Hearing her scream out my name in pleasure is now a goal I can't wait to meet. She pulls away from our kiss and her cheeks heat, I have a thing about the pink tinge that now rests upon her. I can't help but wonder if she turns this shade of pink all over her body.

"Hi," I say to her, stupid word for the first one I know, but I am at a loss for words.

"Hi," she repeats back to me, and I like the smile she is wearing at this moment.

"I guess we should get these festivities going, everyone is

watching us to see what we'll do next," I inform her, causing her to look around like she's just realized it's not just the two of us. As she looks back at me she throws her head back in laughter and I want to memorize that sound and carry it with me everywhere I go.

"I guess we should," she declares to me still wearing that beautiful smile upon her face.

I grab her hand and we walk down the aisle, followed by Ghost and who I assume to be her sisters. They all look alike to me letting me know they're definitely kin to each other. As we pass by her parents, her mother is wiping away tears and smiles at us as we pass, her father however is wearing a scowl upon his face. Fuck him! She's mine now, and if I want to kiss her the way I did he has no rights to say differently any longer. She's mine!

The evening drags on, pictures, dinner, cutting the cake and the best part, our first dance. I know what people think when they look at me, how on earth can a biker know how to dance? Easy, my mom use to dance with me in the living room, in the kitchen wherever and whenever the mood would strike her. Mom enjoyed to dance, and I was her sidekick, I learned the waltz when I was only ten years old.

Those are some of the only good memories I have from my hellish childhood and I thank God, every single damn day for those that I do have. The song that plays however isn't one I can show off my waltz moves to…it's Aerosmith's I don't want to miss a thing, but I can slow dance with her cuddled in my arms and that's worth me not showing off my moves.

It's the first time we've gotten a moment alone, I take advantage of that and lay a slight kiss upon her lips. She reciprocates and the next thing I know we're standing still in the middle of the dance floor lost in each other.

I place my hands on her cheeks making the kiss more intimate and personal. I want to show her that she's special and that even though we were forced into this arrangement, she won't be treated as such by myself. I hear whoopin' and cat calls which bring me out of the trance I'm under. I smile at her and she returns the smile, lighting up the room and my heart. How is it even possible that I've only met her a few short hours ago and I already feel the way I do about her?

It's as if she's put some type of spell on my broken, shattered heart and it's waking up for the first time in many years. I have a feeling she's going to be the best thing that's ever happened to me in my life. She was meant to be mine and I am meant to be hers, it's like fate threw us together and I want to treasure this gift it has bestowed upon me.

I grab her hand and walk us back to our table, it's in the middle of the others to where everyone is surrounding us any way we turn. Her family is all behind us and my brothers take up the rest, I notice for the first time that her father brought some of his business associates with him, none I know personally, but from the research we've done I know that they are all dangerous men in their own rights. I make a mental note to find out which ones I need to keep an eye on more than the others. I don't trust these motherfuckers, especially with my wife's protection...*my wife*, God I have a weakness for the sound of that.

Before this day, you would have never heard those words leave my lips, but knowing that my future of bedding the Babes is behind me, I feel as if a chip has been pulled off of me and it doesn't seem so bad now to have only one woman for the rest of my life.

Lizzie

I FEEL LIKE I'M LIVING IN A FAIRYTALE, WHO WOULD'VE thought that the man of my dreams would've been thrown at me, an unwilling bride-to-be. I'm his wife, I'm a *wife*! I'm suddenly anxious to find out how compatible we are with each other, there is an instant connection that I can't wait to explore with him. I feel sparks when his lips touch mine and my heart skips a beat every time he smiles at me. I know this is crazy, before today we didn't even know each other, but it feels like we were meant to be.

I know his life is dangerous, but I know—I can feel, how he'll protect me from everything that could harm me in any way. Am I imagining this? Does he really feel the way I think he does? Only time will tell, but for now I think he does and I'm going with it. When we leave the dance floor and sit at the table, I hear a glass being clinked…I guess it's time for the best man speech, I hope I learn something about my husband other than he's an amazing kisser. I know I don't have anything to compare it too, but I'm honestly grateful that he will be my first everything. I see his best man…Ghost, his vest thing says stand up and smile over at us. I can't help but return his smile, he's a good-looking guy, but the woman attached to him is drop dead gorgeous. I'm guessing this is his woman, they make a great looking couple.

"I met Justice in boot camp, I'd never met him before so imagine my surprise to find out we grew up in the same town. We became fast friends, we had each other's backs even then, and there isn't anyone else I'd rather have mine than him. He's loyal, trustworthy, truthful in all things, but better than that, he's never not been there when I've needed him the most. He's the first person to enter my life that I knew would never betray me or leave when things got tough. He's always stood by me in the best of times and the worst. He's like a brother to me, club aside of course. Blood isn't always what makes a family, it's honesty, courage, and respect. Things my man, Justice here has in spades, I know that he will cherish, be devoted to and respect Lizzie and do everything in his power to never let her down." I can't help but admire the passion these two have for each other. It isn't every day I see that type of bond between two men. He continues on, "Lizzie, I know we don't know each other yet, but I look forward to welcoming you into our family, we are a close bunch of people and are excited to welcome you into the fold." He raises his beer bottle in the air, "to Justice and Lizzie." And all of his club brothers repeat the mantra, I can't hold back the tears as they fall down my cheeks, just like that they've welcomed me into their lives.

Then Genny stands up as my matron of honor, she will be the one delivering their speech on my behalf. "The day my baby sister was born, the heavens opened up and rained sunshine down on our family. Rosa and I were so excited to have a baby to play with and help take care of. She's spunky, ambitious and her heart is so full of tenderness, you can't help but to care for her back. She's so precious to us, and we are looking forward to watching her grow and expand her family, we would like to welcome Justice with open arms and I just have to say, I hope you know what a prize you've been gifted with. Take care of her, hold her dear and respect her and what you will get in return will be worth the struggles you two will face while starting your life together. We love you so much, sissy, enjoy your new path and let it guide you to the happiness you deserve." Both she and Rosa wipe tears from their faces, I stand up and walk into their open arms, I'm going to miss seeing them daily.

"Thank you," I divulge to them.

THREE

LIZZIE

THE WEDDING IS OVER AND AS WE GO TO LEAVE, I AM caught off guard when my father grabs me and pulls me to the side. Justice is watching us as I'm escorted away from him, and he doesn't look happy by the event.

"Don't disappoint me, Lizzie, this joining is important to your family. We need this partnership with them, so do as you're told and watch your mouth young lady." Why doesn't it surprise me that he didn't pull me away to give me his well wishes? It's never about his family or his daughters' happiness, it's about what our unions mean for him.

"I'll behave, Father."

"Damn right you will, you're still my daughter and I can

punish you for your misbehavior, I don't care what your new husband says."

"You won't ever lay a hand on my wife! If you do you won't enjoy the consequences of those actions." I jump hearing Justice behind me, I never heard him join us and for him to hear my father's words embarrass me.

"Watch it, boy, this is my daughter and I can and will still punish her for her disobedience."

"I'm not your boy, and over my dead body will anyone ever lay a hand on my wife and Ol' lady. I'm not playing around, do it and see what I do." I look behind me to gauge the look on his face and notice his brothers are standing behind him. My mother is off to the side and I see a smile on her face. I guess she's happy that someone has the balls to stand up to Father.

"Are you threatening me?" Father asks Justice.

"He may not be, but we are," Wasp, the President says. "She's our family now, and no one touches what's ours, we protect our dearest ones at all costs. You can deal with your family as you see fit, but that doesn't include Lizzie any longer. If you wish to keep that relationship with us, I suggest you leave her be." I'm stunned by their protectiveness over me, I've never had that, and I am suddenly glowing with admiration for this group of men.

I catch Wasp's eye and silently tell him 'thank you,' to which I get a head nod in acknowledgement.

"I feel like you're threatening me, I don't do well with threats, Wasp."

"No threats being made here, just stating facts."

"Fine, let's go," he says to my mother and sisters. He looks over at me with a sneer on his face and points his finger at me. Message received loud and clear, Father, we'll be discussing this at a later date and time, a conversation I'm definitely not looking forward to. I turn around and give Justice a wavering smile in thanks for him standing up for me.

"He will never lay his hands on you...*ever*, understand?"

"I do, and thank you, no one has ever stood up to him for me before. You have no idea what that means to me, I feel safe with you—which is crazy since I don't even really know you," I speak out before I realize the words have left my mouth.

"You will always be safe with me, I will protect you with my life as will my brothers. You have nothing to fear, ever again." I lean up and plant a kiss on his cheek in thanks.

"I can't wait to get to know you, Justice, you are an enigma to me."

"Same here, Lizzie, now let's get out of here so we can start doing just that."

———

Getting on the back of his bike in a wedding dress isn't as easy as it would seem. After he teaches me how to mount his bike, where to put my feet and where I need to watch my leg placement so I don't get burned, isn't exactly the first lesson in biker chick 101 I was looking forward to, but it is what it is. I get positioned to where I'm not flashing anyone, and as I think I'm in the right position, he grabs my legs and pulls me closer to him. There is no space in between our bodies, I can feel the hard ridges of his stomach with my hands and I'm looking forward to feeling them up close and personal with no clothing in the way. My helmet is tight, and the chin strap is uncomfortable, but I'm glad he got me my own, so it fits me like a glove.

His thoughtfulness brings a tear to my eye which I hold back, I'm not the sentimental type of girl, but his actions mean more to me than words can say. We drive for a couple of hours before we stop at a bed and breakfast. It's cute in a Victorian home kind of way, I've never been to one and am looking forward to seeing the inside. I know I sound like a spoiled brat, but when you've had no type of adventure in your life, and are only used to the thing's money can buy, it's really nice to be a part of the quainter things. I adore all of the beautiful, colorful flowers that outline the walkway, it's fresh and clean looking on the outside. The house itself is yellow in color with white shutters outlining the windows, it's beautiful and something I could picture myself living in permanently. I would be keen to have something small and tasteful to reside in and raise children in.

I don't even know if Justice wants children, but I pray that he does because I desperately want to be a mother. I can picture a little girl with braids on either side of her head, I imagine her features, she'd have blonde hair color and piercing blue eyes, or a little boy who is the spitting image of his father. It's a dream that I hope one day will come to fruition, I picture us all out in a back-yard tossing around a ball or playing in a sandbox. Snap out of it girl, you haven't even had your wedding night and you're already dreaming of future children!

"What are you thinking so hard about back there, Lizzie? I've called out your name several times trying to get you to dismount the bike." I hide my head on his shoulders from embarrassment.

"Just thinking about our future and daydreaming a bit. Something you'll come to know about me in the future. I hope you're ready for all of my hopes and dreams, Justice."

"Let's get checked in and you can tell me all about them."

"Okay."

It doesn't take long to get checked in to the honeymoon suite and shown to our room, it's absolutely breathtaking. Before I have a chance to completely admire the room I'm pushed in front of the door with Justice's front to my front, he looks into my eyes and lowers his mouth to mine for a beautifully sweet kiss. That sweetness builds a fire within us and we become ravenous with each other, we can't get seem to get enough. His hand moves behind my head where he grabs ahold of my hair, not to the point of pain but enough to control my movement, and he pulls me closer to him. I'm not sure how either of us are breathing right now since my senses are in overload and all I can think about is that my panties may combust at any time now. He pulls away and looks into my eyes again, his chest is heaving, and I can tell he's trying to gain control of himself.

"Wow," is all I can manage to say.

"I really want to take the time to get to know you, Lizzie, but I need you with everything I am. I need to know though, please be honest and don't be embarrassed, have you ever been with anyone before?" I can tell with his eyes that he really doesn't care either way, but I have a feeling if I haven't he wants to make this special for me.

"No, um…you see, we—meaning my sisters and me, we weren't allowed to be around boys." This is really embarrassing, and I can't look at him when I tell him this, he's not having it though and takes his finger and tilts my head up so I have no choice but to look at him.

"What did I say before, Lizzie? This isn't something to be embarrassed or ashamed of, I'm pleased that I will be the first, and last man, to ever make his way between your luscious thighs. It turns me on more than you'll ever know that I will be the only one, in every way to show you the pleasure our bodies can give us." He leans down and captures my lips in a smoldering kiss, next thing I know I'm being laid down on the bed, how we got here without me realizing it has me astonished. Is it possible to swoon outside of a romantic novel? I know this isn't technically a moment most would find worthy, but to me what he said means everything.

"I can't wait to start learning about my body from the touch of your hands, mouth and….um penis."

"Babe, I don't have a penis, only boys have those, I have a cock or a dick. Here feel," he says as he directs my hand over his rock-hard dick. Why is it I can say cock or dick in my head, but can't verbally say those words?

"You're so big, I don't think this will work. I'm not sure something so huge is meant to go down there," I state, and I mean every word, if he is this big behind clothing, I'm scared to see what size he is unrestrained. I gulp with that thought and must have been loud about it because he throws his head back in laughter. My spell is broken, and I look up at him wide-eyed, asking, "will it really fit?" I need to know—my fear is outweighing my desires.

"Yes baby, I will fit, you were made to take me. I'm not gonna lie to you, the first time will hurt, but I'll do everything in my power to make it enjoyable to where the pain is forgotten. I plan on getting you worked up to where your body craves mine."

"Well then, what are you waiting for?" I ask him, his words already have me needing to feel his body close to mine. He hovers over me and starts pulling down the top of my dress, it's so tight on my top that he has a hard time, so I raise up and allow him to unzip the back. He slowly, but methodically lowers the zipper and the wait and anticipation is killing me. "Hurry," I beg him.

"No," one word, but it tells so much. Once he has my dress lowered and it's sitting at my waist, he then kisses my neck down my collar bone and stopping at the top of my breast. He moves his hands behind my back and removes my strapless bra, it falls into my lap, but I lose my train of thought when he takes one of my nipples into his mouth. This is the first time anyone has touched me that wasn't myself.

"So beautiful," he utters with sincerity in his voice, I was nervous about being bared to him in all my naked glory, but right now I want it all removed. I climb up on my knees causing him to lose his purchase and he grumbles a little about it until he sees what it is I'm doing. "Take it all off," I tell him. He pushes my dress down until it's pooled at my knees, he then pushes me back and rips the dress down my legs and tosses it to the floor in his excitement. I feel myself getting more aroused by his actions than I ever believed to be possible.

He starts removing his clothing and I'm watching him like he's unveiling my most prized gift. Once his shirt and cut as I learned it's called are removed he unzips his pants but instead of removing the offending object he leans back over me and gives me a kiss that stops the world from spinning. I groan in protest when his lips move from mine, he trails his lips between my breasts and works his way down my slightly rounded stomach. I go to cover myself and he grabs my hand uttering out the word 'no' and continues his quest of making me his.

Justice

I CATCH HER HANDS AS SHE GOES TO HIDE HER STOMACH from me, I want nothing interfering with my pursuit to her pussy so I tell her no and hold her hands in mine. I push them to her sides and put pressure on her wrists letting her know in no certain terms I don't want her to move them from that spot. I need complete control right now, if I lose it I'm not sure of how gentle I can be to her for her first time. Once I'm sure she's going to be compliant I travel down to her pubic bone and inhale her scent, it's calling to me and I need to eat that pussy now, it's not something I've got a lot of experience in, but I want to make her fly.

I grab one side of her white lacey thong in my mouth and pull it down, she raises her hips and I move to the other side and repeat the action until I have them past her ass and hips. Then I grab the crotch area with my teeth and pull them down her legs, all the while I'm looking into her eyes. I want her to see what she's doing to me, I've never had this type of attraction to another woman and I can't wait to feel her for the first time.

As I make it past her feet I put her panties in my jeans pocket to keep them as my own personal souvenir. One I will treasure until the day I draw my last breath, the day I finally meet my maker. I've had some close calls, but that bastard hasn't gotten me yet, and I plan to live a full life with Lizzie at my side. I don't want an open-ended marriage like I thought I would, no I want her and only her till my dying day.

This almost snaps me out of my sex-induced fog, but I quickly find myself drawn back in by her whimper of anticipation. I slowly kiss up one leg then repeat the process with her other one. I do this until I make it to her center, I lay a kiss on her clit and she responds by raising her hips up to try and get more. Next, I take my tongue and run it from bottom to top and grab her engorged clit with my lips and suck it into my mouth causing the most erotic of sounds to leave her lips.

Those sounds drive me on and I begin to make a full course meal out of her. I lick, suck and kiss her bringing her to unadulterated lust, I insert my tongue inside of my delicious treat until she comes, and I eagerly swallow every bit of her essence. Once I've drowned my taste buds with her sweet release, I climb my way up her body all the while removing my jeans and placing tiny kisses on her body. My body is full of sexual tension and is in need of a release, but I'm trying to be patient and force it upon myself.

All I want to do is slam inside of her, but I know that isn't what is appropriate for a lady's first time. I want to give her so much pleasure that the pain is an afterthought. Once my jeans are removed I lay my body over hers and caress her breasts. They are the perfect size and fit my hands just right, nothing overflowing and not too small. She was made to fit me, all of me, I just have to show her now how right our bodies are for each other.

Knowing I need to make sure she's truly ready for me and my size, I move my hand down and find her and I insert first one finger then two. I find her g-spot and make slow circular motions on it which causes her to detonate rather quickly. I can't put it off another minute, but fearing for her pain I ask her, "Slow and easy or quick and fast?" as I line myself up with her opening.

"Fast and quick," she says breathlessly. I use the drop of cum at the head of my dick to add to her lubrication, I insert the head of my cock inside of her and feel her body tense. I take my thumb and make circular motions on her clit and apply a little pressure, she wraps her legs around my hips and I move a little further inside of her. I rock my hips back and forth putting myself a little further inside of her. I lean down and wrap my lips around one of her nipples causing her to moan. "Yes, please," she cries out.

It's now or never and the latter isn't an option, so I slam inside of her and lay my body over hers waiting for her to grow accustomed to my size. She's so tight that my eyes cross while I wait for her body to be ready to accept what comes next. I feel her relax and her small whimpers of pain subside, and she pulls me closer to her. "Now, please move now, I'm alright."

"Only if you're sure," I say through gritted teeth.

"I'm completely sure, please move." I grab one of her legs and move it closer to her head for a deeper angle, she lets out a moan of pleasure as I get deep inside of her. I let out my own moan of appreciation then my hips take on a life of their own and I start making love to someone for the first time in my life. I slowly rock back and forth—the friction is growing with my every movement.

"Fuck me, beautiful, you feel so good gripping my cock in your pussy."

"Mmmm…faster, please more."

Giving into her demands isn't a hardship seeing as it's taking everything I have to move slow and steady. I pick up the rhythm and slam myself into her with every downward thrust. Faster and harder I move my hips until I can feel the pressure in my balls and feel a tingling sensation at the base of my hips, a sure sign that I'm fixing to blow my load, but she needs to get there before I do. I use more pressure with my thumb and go faster wanting to help her reach her own orgasm. Just as I've about given up that she will reach her peak she wails out and clamps down on me.

"Yes!" she screams out as I call out her name and it takes everything I have not to flop down on her. I lay down and put my arms around her and roll us on our sides facing each other. "Can we do that again?" she asks me, and I can't help the rumble of laughter as it leaves me.

"Yeah, beautiful, we can do that again, just give me a minute to recover," I answer with a smile on my face. Oh yeah, this is going to be an adventure of a lifetime.

FOUR

LIZZIE

WE HAVE SEX TWO MORE TIMES BEFORE MY BODY IS FULLY satisfied and satiated. I'm nearly asleep when I hear him come back into the room from the bathroom, saying, "Beautiful, come on I ran you a bath, you're gonna need it to help with the soreness."

"Don't want to move."

"You don't have to, I'll carry you." With the last word spoken I feel my body lifted up from the bed. Not wanting to fall I immediately put my arms around his neck and hold on for dear life. No one has carried me anywhere since before I learned how to walk.

"Justice, put me down, I'm too heavy, we're going to fall," I squeal out.

"You're light as a feather, beautiful, no way I'd ever let you fall. If you're in my arms you're safe from anythin' bad coming your way." I adore the way he sometimes misses the 'g' and 's' at the ends of his words. They make his way of speaking something I'll never forget, he's not proper and it turns me on to no end.

"You're just saying that because you're so muscly."

"Damn you're so fuckin' cute…muscly, didn't even know that was a word until now."

"It's not, I made it up, but it describes you perfectly. My muscle man, don't you think it's the perfect word for your body?" I ask him curious to hear what he'll say.

"Hot, sizzlin', fuck worthy, those are a few of the words I'd personally use," he teases me.

"I like this."

"Like what beautiful?"

"This sexy, funny banter we have going on…tell me we'll always have that."

"We will, beautiful, always and forever. We may get mad at each other sometimes, say something that will hurt the other's feelin's or do something extremely stupid…I expect that more from me than you by the way, but we will always make up and we will forever have our fun times. The good will always outweigh the bad, I'll make sure of it." I look into his eyes and let him know with my look how much his words mean to me.

"The good times and the bad times, they will all counter each other, I've never had a relationship before, Justice, but I will give it everything I've got. That's a promise I will make to you and I am nothing if not a woman of her word."

"Same here, beautiful, except I'm a man of my word. I will disappoint you sometimes, but I promise it will never be intentional. I also have never been in a relationship, so this will be a learning process for both of us."

"I can work with that," I inform him truthfully, because you can't expect someone to give more than what they have inside of them to share. I don't expect anything less than, or more than we have to share.

———

I WAKE UP THE NEXT MORNING AND STRETCH OUT MY sore limbs. Thank goodness for Justice's forethought to get me in the tub. I notice the bed beside me is empty, I'm disappointed but can't help but think back to our bath. He washed me, caressed me and took such good care of me—heart, body and soul. No one has ever tended to me the way that he did, and it makes me wonder if it was a onetime deal, or if I'll be privileged to get that kind of treatment on a regular basis. I look over as I hear the door open to our room and notice he has his hands full with a tray of food. The first thing to hit my senses is coffee, the nectar of the Gods.

"I was trying to get back before you woke up, beautiful," he says to me as he sets the tray down on the bed next to me and climbs in to join me. First thing I do is head for the coffee, I add my sugar and creamer and with my first sip I moan out my enjoyment. There is nothing like waking up with a fresh brewed cup of godliness, I look over and see that Justice's eyes are glazed over with lust.

"What?" I ask in between sips.

"You keep making sounds like that, beautiful, and our breakfast will be cold before we ever even touch it."

"Ummm…okay, what noises?"

"The noises you make when I'm deep inside your delicious body." With those words I can't help but rub my thighs together. "Eat," he tells me, "I don't want you eating a cold breakfast, I have plans today and at the end of it, when we come back to the room, I want you famished, but for something other than food." I feel a flood in my panties as my body instantly reacts to his words.

"Are you planning on feeding me all day long, Justice?"

"Among other things, beautiful." Cue my nipples going rock hard, joining the leak in my lower region. Fuck me, how am I supposed to make it a whole day when he says things like this to me?

"What are we doing today?"

"It's a surprise…eat up, we have a long day of fun and adventure waiting on us." Not wanting to look like a pig eating from their trough in my rush to see what he has planned, I force myself to take my time and chew everything that enters my mouth thoroughly.

———

ONCE I'M DRESSED AND WE GET ON THE BIKE AND HEAD out of town, I'm pleasantly surprised at how at home I feel sitting behind him and enjoying the wind on my face. When we pull into our first stop of the day, I'm surprised at where he's taken me. We're at a custom bike shop and I see apparel in the window. This place is huge, and I know it's not a chain, because I've never heard of them before.

"What are we doing here?"

"Need to make sure you have everything that will keep you safe on the back of my bike, beautiful."

"But I already have a helmet."

"That's not enough, you need leathers, riding boots and whatever else I feel like buying for my beautiful wife while we're here." Well, okay then, how can I turn him down? He looks so cute and excited to get me things. He's bouncing around like a kid in the candy store waiting on me, I grab his extended hand and let him lead me from the parking lot. He opens the door for me and as we enter he places his hand at my lower back and follows closely behind me. I don't know if he's staking a claim on me, or if he's just wanting to have his hands on me at all times. We look around the store for a few minutes before a salesman joins us.

"Justice my man, it's good to see you again, it's been awhile."

"That it has, Hunter, good to see you too. Let me introduce you to my wife, Lizzie."

"Nice to meet you, ma'am."

"Nice to meet you too, and please call me Lizzie." He reaches out to shake my hand and Justice lets out a low growl. I look back at him in shock, I've never heard that sound from another human being in my life.

"I don't like another man touching you," he announces.

"But you let your brothers touch me," I state with amusement in my voice.

"That's different."

"Oh yeah, how so?" I'm caught off guard at the laugh that leaves Hunter.

"Don't worry man, I'm not interested in your wife," Hunter tells him through his laughter.

"Good to know, we're new so just don't touch her, alright?"

"You got it, man, no touching, she's off limits." He backs away with his hands held up in surrender. I mean are we for real here? I feel like I'm in a caveman showdown.

"Damn fuckin' straight she is." I roll my eyes at his male macho business, but I must admit, I am fond of the fact that he is acting like this. It lets me know that he has a lot of the same feelings I am experiencing as well.

"What'cha needing today, Justice?" Hunter asks him and then looks at me like I'd know what we're specifically shopping for.

"Need to get my *wife* some riding gear, the normal, leathers, boots…etc." God the possessiveness in his voice makes me all giddy inside like a school girl with her first crush.

"You got it, man, let's head on over to the lady's section and see what we have that you would like." And that's how we spend the next two hours, shopping, laughing and loading me up in apparel.

Next stop is at a men's and women's spa. I look at him in surprise, this isn't anything I remotely imagined doing today.

"I thought you might enjoy this," he voices to me.

"What are we having done? I already got my nails and waxing done before the wedding." He rumbles his appreciation for the waxing which causes me to laugh. He expressed to me repeatedly last night how he enjoyed no hair down there while he was taking care of business. Making me wish we were back at our room we have for the weekend and enjoy that venture again...now. As we stand here I rub my thighs together. Once again, it feels like that's all I've done since waking up this morning.

"Patience, beautiful, anticipation will make it so much sweeter when I sink deep inside of you." Someone help me, this day needs to hurry up and be over with! After we've been massaged, I've had a facial and we eat the lunch provided for us, we make our way back to his bike.

"Are we heading back yet?" I look up at him begging with my eyes for him to say yes.

"One more stop. I want to get you a gun, so we can get you your concealed handgun license."

"Wait, what, why?" I've never held a gun and don't have a desire to start now. I shiver at the thought of having one on my person at any time.

"Listen, the life we all live, it isn't roses and sunshine, you need to be able to protect yourself if I'm not around and a situation comes up."

"What kind of situation will come up that would cause me to have to shoot someone?"

"Beautiful, you've grown up in this lifestyle, do I really need to answer that question?"

"Yes, yes you do, because I must've been sheltered more than I thought. My mom and sisters don't have guns. They've never had a need for one."

"Damn your dad for not making sure you're protected and know how to take care of yourself! I won't take any chances where you're concerned...now no more talking and let's go in, if you feel this needs further conversation we'll do that once we get back to our room." Umm... that's not what I want to do when we get back, so I'll let this subject drop...for now. I end up with a Beretta PX4 Storm Compact which is a 9mm and is small enough that it will fit in my purse perfectly. He even had it customized for me with a pink grip with a diamond pattern design ingrained in it. The design is perfect for me, and I like it already and can't wait to pick it up tomorrow and practice shooting it.

Once we make it back to the room, he asks me if we need to finish our conversation from earlier and I respond by jumping in his arms and kissing him. Hint taken, he reciprocates, and we end up in bed ravishing each other...about damn time.

FIVE

JUSTICE

As we pull back into the clubhouse, I can't help but feel disappointed that it won't just be Lizzie and me as it has been all weekend. Our honeymoon was cut short when I got a phone call from Wasp letting me know I was needed back home. So, after packing up, and going to pick up Lizzie's gun, we headed straight back. I feel bad because I notice as we walk into the club Lizzie is walking funny. After our first time, I didn't take it easy on her and then on top of it I threw her on the bike for a long ride home.

"Beautiful, when we get inside I'm gonna get you settled in our room and I want you to draw yourself a bath and relax for a while, so I can check in with the guys and see what's going on...yeah?"

"That sounds heavenly," she retorts with a smile directed my way. I don't think I will ever tire of seeing it brighten up her face. I drop our bags and get her settled. Once I'm positive she'll be fine on her own with how tired she is, I go out in search of everyone. The place was dead as we walked through which means they must be in a meeting and couldn't wait for me. I walk into the room announcing myself the only way I can do and get away with.

"What's up bitches?" I inquire of my brothers as I bang the door open and make my presence known.

"Swear to God, one day you're going to get your ass shot coming in here that way," Wasp informs me, "you could just enter like a normal person you know."

"Now where's the fun in that, Prez?" I ask smartassly.

"Take your seat and shut the fuck up."

"This sounds serious," I state as I sit down and join my brothers.

"It's very serious, I got a call from Kid this morning, seems they're in some hot water out that way and they've asked for some of the single men to head out and help them. However, your special set of skills will be needed to help them out with this situation," Wasp catches me up on the discussion that was taking place when I entered.

"Wanna tell me what's up?" My attitude turns from one of a joking matter to business in seconds. My special skill sets vary, to get away from my parents as quickly as possible after I graduated high school, I joined the Army. I became a Ranger and let's just say that my training is classified.

"Seems that they're still having issues with drugs being sold on their streets and are having a hard time nailing down who is making the shit and who's actually behind the scenes. We need you to go in there and help them nail down this new organization and put an end to them. We promised that town when we moved in that we'd help get their streets clean and keep them that way."

"Will Lizzie be safe?" That's the only thing that matters to me right now.

"As safe as any of the other Ol' ladies that are there. Nothin's guaranteed, but we secured that place like the White House. No one can get in or out of that property without alarms sounding off. It's wired and gated, we wouldn't send you there if we weren't sure she would be as safe as we can make things for her," Wasp tells me looking me in the eyes. I wasn't around when they set up Templeton, I was still in rehab recovering from being shot while rescuing Bristol and Lil' bit from Kori's deranged father.

"I'm there, you know I'd never let any of you down." I'm just wondering if I should call Lizzie's dad, he has plenty of back-up for us if need be.

Before I can voice my opinion, Wasp continues, "We've contacted Lizzie's dad, advised him of the situation, and since he doesn't live too far from Templeton he's offered to assist should the occasion arise." I swear this man has ESP or something, he always knows what I'm thinking and is ahead of me at almost every single damn step.

"I swear you've got some psychic in you somewhere, I was just about to ask if I should call him for help."

"He and his daughters aren't close, as he relayed to me, but he would kill any person who caused them harm or be of any threat to any of them."

"At least he gives a shit, I wasn't sure with the way he acted at the wedding."

"Isn't that the truth? I don't know how long you'll be gone for so pack accordingly, you can take the club truck and pull your bike with the trailer. That way you're prepared with enough things to last you awhile. Knowing how women are, she'll probably have you load up her entire wardrobe, which is a lot let me tell you. It was delivered while y'all were gone. It took several loads to bring it all in and put away. We didn't touch her girly shit, but the boys were all complaining about the amount of shit your Ol' lady has. Good luck with that, brother," he tells me with laughter in his voice.

"I bought her more while we were away, she didn't bring a lot with us since we took the bike, but what she did have wasn't made for riding. Let's just say she now has gear, and looks smokin' hot in her new clothes."

"Oh shit, he's got that look," Tic says and every one of these fuckers laugh.

"What look might that be?" I can't see my face, so I'd like to know.

"That you're in lurve," Ghost says making googly eyes, and pushes out his lips as if he's going to blow me a kiss.

"You gonna kiss me now, Ghost? Gotta say, didn't realize Bristol wasn't satisfying all of your needs. But if you must, I'll bend over, and you can kiss my ass."

"Fuck you, Justice, my Ol' lady keeps my lips plenty busy."

"TMI, motherfucker, she's like a sister to me."

"Hey, you started it," he inserts.

"And now I'm ending it," Wasp tells us, shutting us both

up. What can I say, sometimes we like to act like immature teenagers, but it keeps things fun and interesting. "Go talk to your woman, Justice, meeting is adjourned," he says slapping the table letting us know discussion and play time is officially over.

———

ONCE I MAKE IT TO OUR ROOM, I WALK IN AND SEE Lizzie is fast asleep. She's curled up in a ball in the middle of the bed. A smile crosses my face knowing that I'm part of the reason she's so utterly exhausted. I wonder if she suffers from insomnia, if she does I wouldn't mind helping her find sleep on a nightly basis. A man's job is to care for his wife, and that's one job that wouldn't be a hardship conquering. I decide that while she's sleeping I'll head in the bathroom for a quick shower. I don't know my Ol' lady all that well yet, so I'm not sure how to break the news to her that we'll be moving for an undisclosed amount of time.

She hasn't even spent one night here yet and I'm already moving her. It would be different if I was taking her to our home, something I don't own as of yet. Now that the thought's entered my mind, I'm wondering if I shouldn't go ahead and have the girls get started on finding us a few to visit once we return.

Once I finish with my shower and shaving I walk back into the bedroom to get dressed. Once I've got my jeans on and am pulling my shirt over my head I hear her moving around in the bed. I'm not going to do anything with her since we've been going at it non-stop since our wedding night, but I wouldn't mind holding her while we have the talk about plans for the next several months. I climb in next to her and lay on my back before I pull her body on top of mine.

"Hmm…" is all she articulates.

"Have a good bath and rest, beautiful?"

"Yes, I feel so refreshed and ready to get up and meet everyone I didn't get the chance to at our wedding."

"You ain't missing nothing," I tell her jokingly.

"So, you don't want me to meet them?" she asks me with her eyebrows drawn back like I've offended her somehow.

"I absolutely do, but we need to talk before I go and introduce you to those you didn't get a chance to meet."

"Is everything okay, Justice? You have me worried with the tone in your voice."

"Everything is golden, Lizzie."

"Well, you called me Lizzie instead of beautiful, so I'd say everything isn't great."

I break down and tell her about my brothers out in Templeton, about the trouble they've found themselves in and how my help is needed to get the situation under control and detained.

"Could you tell me why it's so important for you to be there and what it is exactly they think you can do to help them absolve this issue?" Listen to her and her fancy words…God I enjoy hearing her speak.

"Let's just say I have special training."

"Care to elaborate on this special skill set you have?"

"I told you bits and pieces about my childhood, but what I didn't tell you is the second I graduated high school I joined the Army. I did well and moved on and was accepted for the Rangers."

"Aahh …" she gasps, "you're an Army Ranger?"

"Was beautiful, was—am not now, but I have the training needed to get inside and get some intel, I am the best at not being seen or heard, I can track better than anyone in our club and I have resources that may be needed during this mission."

"Mission huh, sounds like you still have some Ranger in you soldier," she teases me.

I appreciate her sense of humor, decide she's in a playful mood I want more of, so I begin tickling her. I have her underneath my body and that quickly morphs into something else as my body responds to her nearness. I know I told myself I wasn't gonna take her again, but she's so fuckin' sexy and adorable that I can't help myself. We begin to kiss, and I remove our clothing as quickly as I possibly can. I wonder how long I will crave her the way I do?

A couple rounds of sex, six orgasms later and we pack up and are ready to hit the road. I'm gonna stop in at the local diner on our way out of town and feed her for our two-hour journey to join my other brothers at their new clubhouse.

———

WHEN WE PULL UP TO THE TEMPLETON COMPOUND, I roll down my window and tell the new prospect to inform Kid that I've arrived.

"Prez says to pull on up and they'll be out to help you unload. Your room is set up and ready to go," he informs me.

"Thanks, and you are?" I ask because his name isn't sewn onto his cut, letting me know he's new to the game.

"West," he tells me.

"Appreciate it, West, be seeing you around," I convey to him as I roll through the opening gates.

"I'm glad to see they take security seriously here, I was worried when you told me it was new. I wasn't sure they'd be set up already."

"We've learned some hard lessons the last few years and security is our top priority, that and our women's safety," I say, squeezing her hand which has been in mine the entire trip.

"You ready to meet the rest of my family? They were dealin' with shit here and didn't make it, I think you'll get along well with the Ol' ladies."

"I hope they're more inviting than the women of your club were," I hear her mumble. I'm stunned, I guess I didn't realize they weren't as welcoming as I thought they'd be.

"You'll need to explain that to me once we're settled for the night," I tell her, opening up the door so I can get out.

"It's not important, pretend like you didn't hear that," she says, looking out the passenger window.

"That's not how this works, beautiful," I tell her. I walk around the front of the truck and to her side and open her door to help her out.

"Thanks," she says, placing her hand in mine. Once I have her out of the truck, I place a kiss on her forehead.

"I don't want you stressin' about anythin', give it time and you'll fit in. They won't be able to help but like you. You have an amazing personality and are easy to get along with. They just haven't had the chance to get to know you. Give it time, for me," I give her my puppy dog eyes and she sighs...score! Gets her every damn time.

"I will, Justice. I just worry that I'm the odd man out. I just hope the actions of my father don't punish me in the long run." I understand what she's saying, but I don't feel that they'll hold anything against her. I'll talk to Bristol, I know she'll help her out, Kori too. Ashton is another story all together, she's protective of all of us, and most likely sees my Lizzie as the enemy. If it becomes too much, I'll have to say something to the guys.

"Stop makin' out in my parkin' lot and get your asses inside!" I hear Kid holler out.

"Hold your damn horses, we're coming!" I call back out.

"I've got your horse swingin' right here," he beckons back, holding himself between his legs.

"Watch it, asshole, my wife is standing right here and there's no need to scare her off or blind her for a life-time," I playfully reply.

"You're just scared she'll know there's bigger and better out there and leave your ass," he adds. I grab Lizzie's hand and walk her up to where Kid is standing. After I punch his shoulder and we exchange pleasantries, I introduce him to my wife.

"Kid, this is my wife, Lizzie. Lizzie, meet my friend and the President of the Templeton charter, Kid."

"It's nice to meet you," she answers, taking Kid's outstretched hand. He grabs hers and pulls it in and kisses the back, right above her knuckles.

"Watch it, fucker," I playfully growl. I have nothing to worry about when it comes to my brother and trying to put the moves on my woman. He's a very happily married man and father of the demon twins. At their young tender age, they are hell on wheels and it's hard to keep up with their antics. We adore them anyway, no matter what mess they seem to get into and cause. They take after their father on that aspect of things, so who can blame them for what DNA flows through their body.

"Come on, let's get you two settled in your room, Riley expects the two of you to come to the house for dinner. She's been preparing all day, she's excited to see you and meet your wife."

"Sounds good, we could use a good home-cooked meal. We ate out a lot on our honeymoon and didn't get a chance to eat at the club before we left to head here." Lizzie nods her head in agreement, but she looks exhausted. "Let me get her down for a nap and I'll come down and talk to you and set our plans in stone."

"Prospect!" he thunders out.

"Yes, sir," the young kid comes up to us.

"That's Prez to you, not sir. Get Justice and Lizzie up to their room and hand them the key. While they're getting settled, I want you to bring up their luggage."

"Yes, sir…um, Prez sir," he replies. "Come with me and I'll show you where Prez has you set up." We follow the kid up the stairs and down the hallway. It seems we're being led to the officer quarters if memory serves me right.

"We made sure you had one of the rooms that had a bathroom attached," he tells me unlocking my door.

"We appreciate that," I counter, and know that with as quiet as Lizzie is being, she's fixing to crash while standing on her feet. I hand him my truck keys and send him down for our belongings, while he's gone doing that, I get Lizzie settled in bed. "I'm not going to leave until our things are brought up, after that, I'll lock the door while you sleep and head on down and meet with Kid."

"Sounds good, I just need an hour to recharge then I'll be good to go," she expresses around a yawn. "Love you," she mumbles as she falls into a deep sleep.

"You, too," I mutter. I'm still unsure of myself when I say these words to her, I do adore her, but I fear that I'm lying to her when I make these declarations. Is it really possible to be in love with each other after such a short amount of time knowing each other? I'm protective of her, that's a known fact, and I feel my heart beat faster each time she smiles at me. Affection has always been a foreign concept to me, I have been passionate about many, but I've never experienced being in love...so I question on if that is what I'm indeed feeling.

———

ONCE I HAVE US SEMI-SETTLED, I HEAD DOWN TO THE bar and grab a beer before I seek out Kid. Locating him in his office, I bang on the door and wait to be called in.

"Enter!"

"Is that how you welcome visitors here? Gotta tell you, it needs some work, man."

"Shut the fuck up, Justice."

"Not my style," I comeback and cause him to smirk.

"Some things never change," he playfully states. This time, I'm the one who smirks at him.

"Tell me a little about the issues you're having?" I request, sitting down and putting my feet up on his desk.

"Does this look like your home?" he questions me.

"Nope, but I don't mind making myself at home while going over the issues with you." Might as well get comfortable, because I know we're gonna be here for a bit.

"It's gonna be fun having you around," he deadpans.

"Always, brother. I'm the life of the motherfuckin' party!" I shout.

"If this is a party, I hate to see what happens at a funeral when you're around," Ryder states coming into the room. We all somber at those words, wasn't too long ago we buried King and he's sorely missed by all of us. Not a day goes by that I don't pick up my phone to call him and ask for his advice…especially with me now being married.

"I miss Dad every day," Kid tells us. "I could really use his guiding hand at a time like this."

"We're all here for you, whatever you need, you're not alone in this," I state, trying to comfort him the only way I know how.

"Wasp and Tic have been instrumental, but there's a loss I feel every day."

"That's understandable, man. He was a man who you can't help but miss on a daily basis," I respond, losing myself in my own misery.

"Okay, enough of this shit, I need your help," Kid informs me.

"Yes, down to business," Ryder states.

"We got rid of our last threat, just to have another one pop up. They could've at least waited six months, so I could get my house in order. Anyway, it's some punk ass, low-life drug dealers who've decided to move into my territory. So far, they've hidden their lab so far under the radar that we can't find it. We know two of the key players, I have files on them that I'll hand you once we're done here so you can do some of your own research."

"Do we know if they're low-level or do they have support from someone with power?" I ask, happy that we've gotten down to business.

"They're being financed by someone. These are kids, Justice. No older than nineteen I'd say. No way they have the kind of green it takes to run this type of organization."

"They're banking," Ryder adds. "Not just a little either, they're driving around in Land Rovers and Mercedes and shit. No way a kid on the streets can make that kind of cash without financial backing. No, someone's messin' with us and using these kids as the bait. We just need to go fishin' and find out who it is they're workin' for."

"Sounds as if I'm not gonna have a lot of free time on my hands. Think the ladies will be willin' to step up and help Lizzie find her bearings? She's new to club life, as you well know. I don't think she'll fit in unless someone offers to show her the ropes."

"Now you know Sadie, Riley and Skylar are gonna be all over that shit. Kaci too, but she's a little busy with some client that seems to be takin' up a lot of her time. Trust me, it's been a thorn of contention between her and Travler." I roll my eyes, because Trav is not only protective of his woman, but he's got a jealous streak a mile long. He worships that woman, she's his world and he holds her close, but not too tight for fear of pushing her away.

"How are they holdin' up?" I probe, curiously. Those two had this push pull thing going on until Travler finally got his foot out of his ass and did something about it. He manned up, but not too long later knocked her up. Kaci had a hard time adjusting to motherhood in the beginning with their son's rough start, but from what I hear she's grasped it and is a damn good mother.

"They're doing really good, they're practically insepara-ble, which is why I think he's having such a hard time with how demanding her new client is."

"They'll figure it out," I enlighten him, because I can see the worry etched on his face.

"All these damn women keep us on our toes," Ryder chuckles, then points at me, "just you wait, that spitfire you married will make you question everything you thought you knew."

"Already has," I inform him.

"Check out the information in the folder and we'll pick this up tomorrow. You've gotta go get your woman up and ready, because Riley is blowing my damn phone up. She's anxious to meet your bride, might wanna give her a heads up," he laughs out.

"Will do, are you and Skylar joining us?" I prod Ryder.

"Not tonight, man. She has a final tomorrow that she's studying for…maybe another time."

"Let's make it soon, I'd like Lizzie comfortable with as many of you as possible before I become scarce around here."

"You got it." I walk out of the room, ready to see my woman. I can't believe how much I missed her, and I was only away an hour, tops.

SIX

LIZZIE

I SLOWLY OPEN MY EYES WHEN I FEEL A RUSH OF WARM air blowing in my ear.

"Time to rise and shine, beautiful." I stretch my body, slowly waking up. My limbs are sore from all of the driving and riding I've been doing. I open my eyes and the glorious sight that is my man greets me.

"Hey, how long was I out?" I question.

"Not long, but we need to shower and get dressed. Dinner at Kid's tonight, I can't wait for you to meet Riley and the two spawns they made."

"Spawns, that's kind of a mean terminology for their children, don't ya think?"

"No, they're twins and give the meaning double trouble

a whole new category. You'll be runnin' for your life once you are alone with them for more than two minutes."

"They can't be that bad, Justice. They're just kids." He laughs at me, and it makes me a little nervous. Seriously, kids are kids, they are innocent and sweet.

————

WE HAVEN'T BEEN THROUGH THE DOOR MORE THAN TWO minutes when the most adorable children come up to me.

"Who're you?" the little boy asks me.

"I'm Lizzie," I respond.

"Are you the bitch my uncle had to marry?" the girl asks me, and I know my jaw has dropped and is possibly touching the floor.

"Jayna! Where did you learn that word?" I see Kid look anywhere but at his daughter and I can see the laughter that he's holding in. Okay, I can admit when I'm wrong and Justice was right about these two. They are most definitely a handful!

"I heard Uncle Ryder telling Daddy that she was a bitch," she pouts. My eyes are so wide I'm afraid they're going to explode out of my face.

"Now wait a minute!" Kid hollers out, "that isn't how that conversation went," he declares defending himself.

"Then how exactly did it go?" Justice rumbles out.

"I'd like the answer to that one too," Riley says, giving Kid a dirty look with her hands in fists dug into her waist.

"Maybe we should have this conversation a little later when nosey there isn't present," he expresses, pointing at his daughter.

"We'll be having that conversation alright, brother," Justice glares at Kid. I feel really uncomfortable right now, and it's the first time I've heard that tone come from my husband and it's got me a little off kilter. My entire body shudders from the thought that this conversation may not be pleasant, it also makes me wonder what everyone truly thinks about me. I hope they're willing to give me a chance to show them who I am and not who they presume me to be.

Justice squeezes my hand and it brings me out of my thoughts. "Everything's going to be fine, relax." That's easy for him to say, my friends aren't sitting around talking shit about him and calling him names.

"Jake, Jayna, you two go on to your rooms until we call

you out for dinner," Kid instructs them, and they scurry off. Looks like they listen to their dad at least.

"Lizzie, Riley and I would like to apologize to you on behalf of our daughter. She overheard Ryder and I joking around about our man, Justice here gettin' himself a bitch. It wasn't meant to be disrespectful or derogative towards you."

"Yes, I apologize on behalf of not only my young child but my big one too," Riley verbalizes to me, patting Kid on his head. She really does see him as one of her children. I hide my mouth with my hand trying to prevent the giggle that wants to escape.

"Woman! Stop patting me on the head like I'm your motherfuckin' pet! I'm not now, or never have been a dog," Riley starts laughing, and I soon find myself joining her.

"Lizzie, why don't you join me in the kitchen, while I finish dinner I'll make you a big glass of wine. With these two and those heathens of mine, you may need it."

"I'll take that glass of wine. I'd offer to help you out, but I've never cooked before. I was actually forbidden to go into the kitchen so I'm afraid I'd be more of a hindrance to you then any help."

"I'll take the company, follow me." I go to walk behind her, but Justice grabs my wrist and stops me.

"Don't leave without giving me those lips," he declares, and I swear I swoon at his words. He leans down as I go up on my toes and our lips meet in the middle. It isn't a consuming kiss, but it's full of passion and fire without the use of our tongues. My face flames when I hear Kid make a whipping sound. I scurry out of the room as quickly as my legs take me.

Justice

"She's not a bitch," is the first thing that comes out of my mouth once my woman leaves the room.

"It wasn't meant in that manner," he expresses.

"I know some of you are having a hard time with the way we were forced into marriage. The thing is, none of you know her story. She's more of a victim in this scenario than I am. I need you all to give her a chance, she's a good woman, and she's now mine, which means she's one of ours. I need you all to stand behind me and support both of us, not be a deterrent in what happens between us."

"You've fallen for her, damn man, you didn't even meet her until your wedding day, and she's already got you?"

"There's things you don't know, things that are not mine to share. I won't dignify your question with an answer. It makes me feel like I'm betraying what I've already started building with her. But if none of you are willing to put the effort into befriending her, you'll be the one's missing out on gettin' to know a special woman."

He runs his hands through his hair before saying, "You are the one we worry about. You're our family, our brother. We are all a little skeptical about what it means for you, for your future. Give us a break, we always have your back. This is an odd situation, one we've never faced before. Give it time. Everyone will warm up to her once they get a chance to speak with her." I nod my head, because what else can I do. I'm not going to sit around and beat my head into the wall trying to get through to everyone.

He's right about one thing, once everyone gives her a chance, she'll gain their loyalty and trust, the way she has me. She's a special person. The sooner everyone sees that, the more she'll feel a part of us and open up more. She's told me some about her childhood, but I have a feeling we haven't scraped the bottom of the barrel…yet.

"Let's grab a beer, I'm sure dinner will be ready shortly."

We grab our drinks and head out to the back porch where Kid catches me up on my brothers, their Ol' ladies and the kids. I feel like it's been a lifetime since I've seen anyone when in reality it hasn't been. When he tells me about Jayna and Jake I can see the pride shinning in his eyes. I hope to one day feel the fondness of a father, Lizzie and I haven't even discussed kids. I wonder if she even wants any? About an hour later we're called in for dinner, the kids are funny when they talk and before I know it the night is over and we're heading back to the clubhouse.

———

THE NEXT MORNING, I FIND MYSELF IN A MEETING, KID has been given more intel so he's catching me up and all I wanna do is head back to the room and bury myself inside of my wife. We stayed up half the night exploring each other and fucking like animals. I can't seem to get enough of her, she's unlike any woman I've ever experienced before. Usually I have no issues dumping them and moving on, but with her, I want her at all times. The way she smiles, how she's always excited and ready to try new things astounds me, she's like an addiction that I can't overcome.

"Earth to Justice," Kid calls out, waving his hands in my face.

"Sorry, zoned out there for a minute," I answer.

"Know that feeling well, brother." And by the smile on his face, I can tell that he does. He and Riley have been together for a long time now, and he still acts like they're a new couple. I can only hope and pray that Lizzie and I still have that effect on each other when we've been together as long and longer than they have.

I get back into the topic at hand and put Lizzie and our relationship to the back of my mind. An hour later, I find myself tracking down my woman. I finally find her shooting pool with Skylar and Sadie. They're all laughing, and I can't help but to stop and watch the smile that graces her beautiful face. She's more carefree now than what she's been—even with me.

"It's a fuckin' amazin' sight isn't' it?" Ryder comes up behind me and asks.

"It's the best to see those smiles on their faces," I retort.

He slaps me on my shoulder, "It just gets better from here." He walks away and heads over towards his woman and I follow his lead. I walk up behind Lizzie and wrap my arms around her waist.

"Need a hand? I can show you some tricks to put those balls into the pockets," I speak softly in her ear and smile from ear to ear when she does a full body shiver. "I can teach you the proper stance and how to hold that stick, beautiful."

"I've never had anyone teach me the right way to shoot some balls," she sassily counters.

"I'd enjoy being able to teach you the art of handling balls," I joke with her.

She winks at me and states, "I do need a proper teacher." Her playful nature gets to me and I nip her earlobe between my teeth and lightly tug at it. She moans, and I go from semi-erect to a full-blown hard on. I push my hips into her ass to show her how she affects me.

"See what you do to me? No one has the ability to make me as stone hard as you do."

"Thank goodness for that, I'd hate to cut a bitch," she says, causing me to burst out into laughter. "What? Don't think that I'd be the type of woman to sit back and let that sort of thing roll off my shoulders! That isn't me, it's best if you learn that now."

"I believe you, baby, and that's a bigger turn on than watching you bending over this table with that stick gliding in and out of your fingers, looking for that perfect shot."

"You just like me bent over with my ass in the air," she

expresses.

"Damn fuckin' right I do, it's such a luscious ass," I run my hands up and down said ass enjoying the way her cheeks fit perfectly in my hands. She was made for me in every way, I've never been so compatible with anyone before. Probably one of the reasons I can't go longer than five minutes without her invading my every thought.

Lizzie

IT DIDN'T TAKE US LONG TO FALL FAST ASLEEP LAST NIGHT once we got back from Kid and Riley's house. Their kids are something else and kept us thoroughly entertained last night, the things that come out of the mouths of kids is something that I'll have to get used to according to my husband. Apparently, this club is drowning in smaller people. I laughed when he actually referred to them in this manner. He says they aren't kids, they're small people who don't act like any children he's ever known.

"Mmmm, morning," I hear murmured into my ear. He's wrapped around me as per usual.

"Morning," I answer back. "Riley invited me to go shopping with her and the other women today, is that okay or do we have plans?"

"I have to head out of the clubhouse on some work, so I'll be gone most of the day. You should go," he informs me. I roll over and he loosens his arms just enough for me to switch positions. Now that I'm looking into his eyes, I can't help but think of what a lucky bitch I am to be married to such a good-looking man.

"Then you'll have to let me up so I can shower, and get dressed. They plan on leaving early," I voice, kissing him under his chin.

"No morning play then," he says, lifting his eyebrows up and down and I want to laugh at how cute he is being, but for some reason I doubt that would be the right thing to do right now.

"You can go one morning without," I tease him.

"I really, really can't," he exclaims.

"Looks like you'll have to, just this once or I'll never be ready in time," I remind him.

"Yeah, yeah," he says, placing a kiss on my lips then releasing the hold he has on me. "You need some money?" I'm shocked as I realize we haven't had the 'money' talk yet. "What's that look all about?" he asks me.

"Well, I was just thinking that we haven't had the 'money talk'," I use air quotes to emphasize.

"Wasn't aware we needed to have that conversation," he responds, "I figured you'd share mine, was I wrong?"

"Well, umm, you see…" I stutter out, "I'm basically loaded, Justice. Neither one of us needs to work, neither do our children, grandchildren, etcetera. I'm sure you are getting the picture." His jaw drops, he goes to say something a couple of times, but I see he's speechless.

"I knew your dad was loaded, but I wasn't aware you were as well," he finally manages to utter. "Wow, babe, I don't know what to say here."

"You don't have to say anything, but just know that you'll never have to financially support me, I can take care of myself and any children we have."

"Fuck, Lizzie, are you trying to unman me here? It's my job, my pleasure to take care of you and your needs. I want to be able to do that for us. I get that your use to living in a certain manner, and I can't compete with that…" I shut him up before he has a chance to finish.

"Justice, I don't need to live the way my parents do. I just want to be happy, and if I've learned anything in life, it's that money doesn't make you happy. It buys things, makes life easier, but it doesn't buy happiness. I'd be happy living in a cardboard box as long as you were there with me. For the first time in my life I feel safe, money didn't do that for me, you did."

"You never felt safe?" he questions me.

"No, not really. My father was, is a hard man. He doesn't show affection, he only knows one way to be, and it isn't niceties. He's mean, and I never knew from one day to the next what I'd do to set him off. My sisters and I walked around on egg shells. For some reason, I always managed to trip that live wire and always ended up in trouble and being punished."

"Explain what you mean by being punished," he declares and has a hard look upon his face.

"Let's table this discussion for another time. We both have things to do today and I'd like to enjoy my time with, and getting to know the ladies, without this conversation weighing on my mind the entire time."

"Fine, we'll table it for now, but Lizzie, we will have this talk. Got it?"

"Got it," I reply. As I go into the bathroom to get ready, I can't help but ponder and worry about how that particular conversation will go. If you're outside of the family and organization, you have no idea how ruthless my father can truly be.

SEVEN

JUSTICE

As I sit and wait on my informant to meet me and share what information he has for me, I can't help but think about what Lizzie had said to me earlier this morning. I know her father is an utter and complete asshole, but I had no idea other than verbally abusing her she suffered in other ways at his hands. I need to make sure we have this conversation sooner rather than later, because I'm feeling murderous at the thoughts that are swimming around in my mind.

Visions of a younger Lizzie appear front and center in my mind. Picturing someone so young and innocent suffering at the hands of someone so much larger than they are makes me want to go to his place and confront him, but I know that it could put the club in a precarious position, and I didn't sacrifice as much as I have to hurt my brothers now.

I mean I'm not suffering or anything, I couldn't be happier in a choice for a wife if I'd hand-picked her for myself. I see a vehicle coming up the dirt road that I'm sitting at and let the thoughts of my wife drift from my mind and get into business mode. My informant is someone I've worked with for years and I trust him wholeheartedly.

"Shaun," I say in greeting when he gets out of his car and meets me at my bike. He knows I won't come to him, he needs to come to me especially since I'm the one paying him for the information he's about to provide.

"Justice, it's been awhile," he replies, sticking his hand out for a shake. In response I grab his hand in mine and squeeze a little while showing respect to him. I have to still show who has the upper hand in this relationship.

"Whatcha got for me?" I inquire.

"Right down to business I see," he nervously chuckles, "the organization you're looking for is up and coming. They are establishing themselves all over Texas, Oklahoma and Arkansas. I can't find out who their backer is, but it's someone loaded. They have taken up residence in an abandoned warehouse just west of where the clubhouse is."

"How far west are we talkin'?" I question.

"No more than five-minutes," he enlightens me. Holy fuck! That's way too close for my comfort. Kid is going to throw a fucking shit fit, and I can't blame him. We need to take these motherfuckers out and make sure they aren't a threat to the family. "Tell me more about what you know about these assholes." For the next hour, we talk about what he's been able to find out and I give him his money when I'm satisfied I have the information I need in order to take this back to Kid and Ryder. But before I do that, I decide to go and see this hideout —personally.

———

FOR A NEW GROUP, THEY ARE VERY ORGANIZED. I PULL out my camera and start documenting things I'm seeing, making sure to get photographs of all of the players I'm witnessing moving around. I wonder which ones of them are key players? Those are the ones we need to remove. Without the bigger fish in the picture to fry, it will be easier to remove them from our area. We'll let our friends in the other states know that they have new players in town, but other than that there's nothing we can do for them. I don't mean that we won't have their backs as they've had ours in the past, I just mean that we can't get rid of our own threat and worry about theirs.

I head back to the clubhouse five hours after I left, loaded down with information and needing to speak with Kid. I haul ass back as fast as my girl will take me, not worrying about any law stopping me because Kid already has an in with the officers here in Templeton and they won't mess with anyone wearing the Rage Ryders' cut. It only takes me a little over ten minutes to arrive at the clubhouse, cementing the fact that they are a little too close for comfort.

The first person I spot once I enter the club is Ryder, walking up to him I ask, "Where's Kid? Need to speak with him as soon as fuckin' possible."

"He's with the twins since Riley and the girls have gone out shopping. They've been gone a long time so I'm sure he's pullin' his hair outta his head by now," he snickers like a fucking teenage girl.

"This can't wait, care to ride with me to his place?"

"Sure thing," he answers, walking towards the door and taking his keys out of his pocket. I briskly head to my bike, ready to get to Kid so we can form some sort of game plan. We mount our bikes and tear out of the parking lot once the gate opens to let us through. When we arrive, and Kid opens the door, the look on my face lets him know that things aren't good and the information I have to share will potentially change things for the club and has the ability to force us into going to war, which means the mother charter will have to get involved in this one. It will take all of us to put an end to the dangerous and offensive new group that is thinking they can come into our turf and try to take over our territory and run drugs, something the club is thoroughly against.

"Fuck!" he says, "come on in, tell me what you've learned." He opens the door wider and Ryder and I follow him inside. I can hear the kids laughing and playing, at least they're in their room and I don't have to worry about being discreet with what I say to him. He leads us into his office, saying, "be right back, need to check on the kids and let them know to stay in their rooms until I come and get them."

"Sounds good," I state, sitting down and getting comfortable because this is going to be a long conversation, and not one I'm looking forward to having. Ryder goes over to the mini-fridge and grabs three beers, he hands me one, puts one on Kid's desk then pops the top off of his own. I open mine up and gulp half of it down in one swallow. By the time I pull the bottle from my lips, Kid heads in and takes a seat grabbing his.

"Okay," he sighs, "talk to me."

"I don't know the name of the group that's moved in," I

begin, "but they are close to the clubhouse, too close if you get what I mean."

"When you say close, how close are we talkin'?" Ryder asks.

"Within walking' distance," I answer back to his question.

"Fuck," they both call out.

"I've got pictures of everyone I saw, took some of plates and cars so we can be on the lookout for those in town. They are a small group, no more than twenty, but they are very well organized which worries me the most. They've got a financial backer with the means to start up not only here, but Oklahoma and Arkansas as well. My informant doesn't know who that is, but he's going to keep diggin' to see what he can come across. I think we need to try and infiltrate them and get someone inside," I put out there, because it's not my decision at the end of the day, but it's one I feel is necessary.

"You may be right, but who do we put in there? Our faces are known in town and there aren't many I'd trust with this assignment," Kid says, pulling on his hair as he stares at his desk. This what he does when he's contemplating how to handle a situation.

"Me," I come back.

"Oh fuck, I don't know, you realize this will put a target on your back, we don't know who the backer is as you've stated."

"True, but you know that I'm the only one around that can pull it off," I emphasize.

"Your Ol' lady is goin' to shit her pants," Ryder expresses.

"Something you definitely need to consider," Kid states, "you've thrown her into this life, a club where she knows no one and then plan on ditchin' her, she's not goin' to take that well, brother."

"Maybe not, but she needs to learn that the club comes first and there will be times I have to leave for extended periods of time to take care of things. You guys will take care of her and the Ol' ladies will be there for her and help her understand and deal," I emphatically counter.

"We need to get it approved with Wasp and Tic first. You're their man on loan to us, it would be disrespectful to not get their okay and give them a heads up," Ryder says to us.

"I'll call them," I state.

"Nah, man, it's my job to talk to them. I'll do it, give me forty-eight hours to devise a plan of action with them and then I'll get back with ya."

"Sounds good, any idea when the women plan on comin' back?" I question him, because for the next few days, I need to spend as much alone time with her to hold us over until we can reconnect.

"They were eatin' a little over thirty minutes ago when I spoke with Riley, they should be back soon," Kid answers.

"Then I'm heading back to the club, I wanna be there when she returns," I stand up and bro hug them. Then without another word said, I leave and head back with worry about how that particular talk will go when I have to tell her the news. I can't share it all with her, but I need to know if she sees me around town, she needs to pretend like she has no clue as to who I am. I don't know who that will be harder on, her or me.

Lizzie

I'VE HAD A BLAST WITH THE WOMEN TODAY, SKYLAR AND Sadie are a hoot and had me rolling in laughter and shedding tears all day with their brand of crazy. When I'm dropped off, a man I've never met before helps me unload my purchases, but he has a cut on, so I immediately trust him. He's a nice guy, who smiled at me and was respectful with the way he spoke with me. I spot Justice immediately in the main room and rush to him, his back is turned to me, so he doesn't see me approach.

"Boo," I breathe into his ear and smile when I see his body shiver.

"Hey, beautiful, did you have fun with the girls today?"

"So much fun," I answer. He leans over, and I meet him in the middle as we share a brief kiss in hello. "I need to go and let the guy who helped me bring things in get them into our room, I'll be right back," I rush out before he has a chance to say anything else to me. I got some sexy negligées and can't wait to show them off to him, one in particular should get his motor revving. When I get to our room I see the man standing there with my bags loading down his arms and I feel terrible for my short stop.

"I'm so sorry," I exclaim to him.

"No problem, ma'am. I'm Malibu, and my Ol' lady is Kassi."

"Oh! I met her today, she's amazing," I reply. As soon as those words are said a huge smile graces his handsome face.

"Yes, she is," I get the door unlocked and he walks into

the room and places my things on the bed. "Well, I need to get home and see if she needs any help, you know, maybe try a few things on for me," he wiggles his eyebrows up and down causing a giggle to escape my mouth.

"You do that, I think you'll like some of her purchases." Before I know it he's left me alone in the room. I unpack my things and put them away. It doesn't take me long to put everything where it belongs so I rush out of the room and go to spend some time with my man. I find him shooting pool with Ryder and Skylar is right there with them. I walk over to her since it's my man's turn to take a shot and sit down next to her.

"Did you already go by your house and put your stuff up?" I probe her.

"I dropped my things off, but I didn't put them away."

"Wow, that was fast."

"That's what I get for purchasing my woman a sports car," Ryder teases.

"Oh, put a lid on it," she tells him, and he rolls his eyes at her words. The adoration these two share, even though their words don't say that to the outside world, is apparent. Since I've spent some time with them, I know that they are truly in love and deeply devoted to each other. They put up a front, but it's so full of shit, and their humor with each other is not the norm, that's for damn sure, but they are the kind of couple I hope to be.

I feel arms wrap around my shoulders and look over to see Justice has perched himself on the arm of the couch. He leans over and gives me another brief kiss before saying, "Missed you, I'm glad you're finally home."

"Me too, it was a long day, but it was loads of fun."

"So you said," he responds with a smile. I appreciate it when that smile is directed at me, I kinda get jealous when it's directed in anyone else's direction. "What's the plans for tonight?" I ask him.

"No plans, just hangin' out with everyone and then later, I plan on ushering you up to our room and having my wicked way with you." My body responds, and I feel my nipples pebble ready and willing to do anything he wants. "I know that look," he leans down and whispers in my ear, "I have a weakness for the way your body responds to me. I can't wait to be buried inside of you later."

"Me either," I breathlessly reply.

"Good to know," he winks at me.

"You're up," Ryder tells him. He gets up and leaves me,

but not before he gently squeezes my shoulder affectionately.

————

SKYLAR STARTED DOWNING SHOTS AND DARED ME TO JOIN her. I am not one to back down from those words, so by the time we're ready to head to our room, I'm staggering and slurring and can't seem to control my steps and my words are slipping out of my mouth with no filter whatsoever.

"Are y…you go…gonna shove that fat cock of yours insid… inside of me?" I finally manage to get out of my mouth. Justice bursts into laughter before picking me up bridal style and carrying me up the stairs. I can't help but admire his strength and don't hide the fact that his display turns me on. "God, you're so…so fre… freaking strong," I slur.

"It's a good thing I am, otherwise you'd be crawling your way up to our room," he chuckles. "I enjoy carrying you, and I especially appreciated the way you let go tonight and had fun with the men and women. They're my family and mean the world to me, so to see the way you're comfortable with them makes me a happy guy."

"Awe," I say, "that's cute," I murmur, laying my head on his shoulder.

"Cute! Woman, I am not cute."

"No? Then what are you?"

"I'm a beast, I'm fucking hot, I'm manly, strong. But I am definitely, most assuredly, not cute!" The serious look on his face makes it hard to hold the laughter inside...so I don't. "What's so funny, beautiful?"

"The look on your face, oh my God it's freaking hilarious."

"Yep, you need to use the restroom, brush your teeth and hit the bed."

"No, no you promised me your cock tonight," I stick my bottom lip out and pout.

"I don't wanna take advantage of ya, darlin'," he tells me.

"But, but I want you."

"I want you too, let's see how you're feelin' in the morning, alright?"

"Fine," I've got my pouting down to a T.

"Turn that frown upside down," he says as we make our way to our door. He juggles me around in his arms as he pulls the key to the door out of his pocket.

Justice

SHE'S FAST ASLEEP BEFORE I EVEN MAKE IT OVER THE threshold of the room. I lay her on the bed and undress her the best I can since she's now snoozing and dead weight. First, I remove her shoes and socks, then unbutton and unzip her pants. I have to lift up her hips, which isn't easy and shimmy her jeans down her hips. Instead of removing her top, I lift her upper body up and slip my hands under her top, I unclasp the back of her bra and lay her back down. I've seen women remove their bra's through their shirt and it doesn't look hard so that's what I do. I struggle with her right one, but by the time I make it to the left I feel like a pro and like I deserve a back slap for my efforts.

She mumbles something that's incoherent, so I pay it no mind and lift the bottom of her t-shirt and pull it off and toss it on the floor where it joins the rest of her clothing. Now, to get her under the covers, I can't figure out a way to do it without disturbing her, so I go to the closet and pull out the extra blanket and toss it over her. Once I have her tucked in, I go and brush my teeth, take a shower and slip into bed buck naked. This has been a long, hard day, and I'm happy to finally put it to rest. It would've been better if I'd ended it buried inside of her.

―――――

I WAKE THE NEXT MORNING FEELING MYSELF BEING sucked deep inside of Lizzie's throat. "Fuck, Lizzie, don't stop," I say to her, while my hips lift up and my dick gets buried deeper. She hums around me and the feeling is one that has my nuts drawing up. "Slow down or I'm gonna come down your throat," I inform her. But this only causes her ministrations to increase in pace, with as close as I am to spilling my seed it makes me wonder how long she'd been at it before I woke up. I holler out her name as I erupt and then my body goes slack. "Damn, baby. You can wake me up like that any time you want," I pant out. She gives me a glorious smile and I can see the pride on her face as she realizes that she made me lose control of my body, which is very hard to do, but she caught me off guard. "Pretty proud of your-self there I see," I state.

"Yes, yes I am," she returns. I watch as she gets up off the bed and bounces her way towards the bathroom. I hear the water running and know that she's brushing her teeth. Any time she goes down on me and gives me head, she always brushes her teeth before she'll allow me to kiss her. She strolls back towards the bed and puts emphasis on her swaying hips which instantly capture the sight of my eyes. They are drawn to her like a moth to a flame, I can't help myself, my woman is sexy as fuck and I enjoy the way her body moves. I don't like it too much when other men look at what's mine, but with a woman who looks like mine does it's to be expected I presume. I've never worried about it in the past, so this is new territory for me.

EIGHT

LIZZIE

I'M STILL NOT VERY SUAVE OR GOOD AT THE GAME OF seduction, but I like to take care of my man and he really seems to enjoy it as well. "C'mere," he says, motioning me over using his pointer finger. I slowly make my way towards him, swaying my hips more enticingly, than that of how I normally walk. His eyes hood in desire, which makes me feel more feminine that I even expected to ever feel. "Do you know what you do to me?" he asks.

"No, what?" I ask him. Once I make it to him he grabs my hand and brings it down to cup his manhood. Holy shit! He's fucking hard as stone and I can't imagine that it feels good, it seems like it would hurt. "Does it hurt?" I ask, not able to hold back my curiosity.

"It does," he replies, "what are you goin' to do about it?"

"What do you want me to do about it?" I sassily question.

"I want you to lick it, suck it, and fuck it," his brass and bold words are still something I'm getting used to, they make me do a full body flush. At the same time, it makes me soak my panties in desire.

"And if I do those things, what are you going to do for me?" I inquire.

"I'm going to eat that pussy and make you see stars by the time I finish with you," he says, licking his lips and I have to cross my legs to apply pressure on my swollen flesh. I stop the moan that wants to leave my lips.

"Since I already 'sucked it'," I use air quotes, "I could just ride you and, um…fuck it," I shyly stammer out. It feels weird to be changing my normal vocabulary so much, but I know it turns him on to hear me say them the way he prefers to hear them.

"Hmmm, beautiful, your mouth is going to get you ridden hard," he tells me, before dragging me between his legs, grabbing my hair from behind my head and bringing me down to his level. He looks into my eyes and then forces my head to meet his and crashes his lips to mine. He has a way of making me weak at the knees, the things this man can do with his mouth are things romance novels are made of.

"I'm gonna lay back, Lizzie. I want you to straddle my head and place your pussy right over my mouth."

"You what?" I ask him. This isn't the first time he's requested this of me, but it still frightens me and makes me wonder if I'm going to suffocate him in that position. I have a hard time letting loose and enjoying myself when he requires this of me.

"C'mon, babe, you know the drill, climb on up." He moves back on the bed and moves the pillows so his head lays flat on the bed. I hesitantly climb up and over him. "Give me that sweet cream," he states, grabbing my hips and pulling them down over his mouth. I cry out the second his tongue lands on me.

"Fuck, fuck, fuck," I chant over and over while he licks me up and down. My hips take on a life of their own when he takes his tongue and circles my swollen clit. My hands clamp on to the headboard so I don't lose my balance. I throw my head back and enjoy everything he's doing to me. I ride his face and he pulls me closer.

"I could eat you out twenty-four-hours a day," he expresses between licks.

"I could find it in my heart to let you," I pant. Before

long, I find myself coming hard. His grip on me tightens as I ride out my orgasm. Even then, he doesn't stop until my body stops quivering from the aftershocks.

Justice uses his hands and feet to crawl out from underneath me. He grabs my hair and unbashfully slants my neck to the left side. He nibbles from my earlobe to my collarbone. "You're tasty everywhere," he whispers, causing tiny pebbles to break out on my skin. "Keep your hands there, scoot your legs back and arch your back," he commands me. I enjoy it when he gets all demanding, and authoritative in the bedroom. It seems I not only like a little pain with my pleasure, but I enjoy for him to go all alpha mode on me as well.

I get in his requested position and I feel him slide further between my thighs. He lines himself up with me and slams home. "This. Right. Here. Is. Mine," he gets out through his thrusts. "Say it, say it's mine."

"It's yours, Justice. Only yours."

"Damn straight," he declares, losing control, and slamming into me. He is deliciously forcing his way inside of me and helping me to accommodate his girth and length. He's my one and only, but somehow, I get the impression he's above average and I'm a lucky woman. He bends over my body and bites down where my neck meets my shoulder. "Every fucking time, Lizzie. Every time I'm inside of you I lose control like a pubescent teenager. Only you have the ability to do that to me," he grits out, between his punishing pace, he slams home with each vicious thrust. He owns me, heart, body and soul.

"I'm gonna come!" I call out.

"Do it, do it now," his hand travels down my stomach and his fingers begin playing with my pussy. I'm not going to last much longer.

"Justice!" I cry out, my body turning to gel.

"Mine, mine, mine," he states, on his last three thrusts inside of me. I can feel his warm seed as it enters my chamber. We don't use condoms, and he's all but demanded I get off of birth control once we get home. It's a discussion I plan on having further with him. I'm not ready quite yet to be a mother, but I'm hoping we can compromise and try in a year or two. I want us to establish us and enjoy some time with just the two of us first.

He falls over to his side, bringing me with him. He spoons me, kissing me lovingly on my shoulders, neck, and temple. "I'm so glad I was the one who was lucky enough to marry you."

"See if you're still saying that in a year," I tease him,

"you haven't had the chance to deal with my stuff spread out on your bathroom counter, my stealing all of the closet space or my bras hanging in the shower to dry."

"Doesn't matter, that's all trivial shit. You as a person are what matters to me, beautiful. Nothing else comes close to making a difference. It's your heart, loyalty, and respect I need. I'm falling in love with you, Lizzie."

"I love you too, Justice. I know it's quick, but your soul calls to mine. We were destined to be together. We were made for one another. Your words are magical," I say, as there's banging on the door.

"What?" Justice bellows out.

"Kid needs you, some more information has rolled in," Ryder hollers back.

"Be there in ten," he responds.

"Will let 'em know." I hear footsteps walk away.

"Guess you're in high demand," I declare, turning in his arms.

"Damn skippy," he voices, rubbing his arms up and down my chest.

"You have an ego, mister."

"Nah, not me," he winks.

"Guess we should get in the shower," I advise him.

"Guessing so," he says getting up. I admire his bare ass and all the muscles he's got not only on his ass cheeks, but his back too. He turns around to see if I'm getting up behind him, "Enjoying the view?"

"Always, it's a great view."

"I know what you mean," he imparts, looking me over. A blush comes over my face, I still am getting used to being looked at as that of a sexy woman, and not my family's nuisance.

We hop in the shower and clean each other up quickly, no time for play. He has a job to do, and he takes his responsibilities seriously. One of the many things I adore about him.

Justice

THIS HAS BEEN ONE CRAZY CLUSTERFUCK AFTER another. Our informants have gone missing, and Kid is having trouble trusting some club he worked with previously. This is not the way to start a brand spanking new charter. We expected some rough patches when we voted on adding a club, but we never realized that some we considered allies of the past, would stab us in the back. Drugs are making their way into the territory, something that we thought we'd put an end to before settling here.

I guess those we trusted made an ass out of us, and we need to nip that in the bud a-s-motherfuckin-p. I have some guys from the old days, they aren't MC, but they are loyal to the bone. I guess it's time to put a call out to them and ask for assistance. We don't have the manpower here to end it...not alone anyways.

I stroll down the hallway, heading to Kid's office to see what he has for me. I'll give him my idea and see if he goes for it. I lift up my hand and rap on the door using my knuckles. "C'mon in," he calls out. Without wasting time, I open the door and walk in.

He holds up his beer bottle in my direction, "Want one?"

"Fuck yeah," I swiftly answer.

"I've got some more information. The drug pushers are new. They aren't in business with the old gang we pushed out before we claimed this territory." So, this new group I've discovered is the issue, I had a feeling which is why I brought it to his attention in the first place.

"No, who are they?" He slides me over a piece of paper, I read over it and whistle.

"Damn man, this isn't good." The Ozzie Walkers are a drug organization that started in Australia, and have made their way into the good old United States of America. They are taking our country by storm, and are a force to be reckoned with.

"This is going to get bloody," Kid utters out loud.

"Ya think?" I smart-assly reply.

"This isn't time for shits and giggles, Justice," he reprimands me.

"Didn't say it was, I was agreein' with you in my own way."

"We need a fool-proof plan," he declares, more to himself than me.

"Got an idea," I start, "if you agree with me, I can get the ball rollin'."

"Please, do share with the class." Well, someone woke up on the wrong side of the bed this morning. Either that, or Riley's holding the pussy hostage.

"I've got these buddies," he doesn't give me a chance to continue before he raises his hand in the air cutting me off.

"What kind of 'buddies' are we talkin' about here?"

"You want me to put together a jacket?" A jacket is a portfolio in biker lingo.

"Why don't you verbally lay it all out for me," he says, jamming his pointer finger into the desk with each word he says. He's more like his dad than I realized.

"Jackson Ramero, the best sniper I've ever seen. He can take any shot, and hit his target if the coordina-tion's are on point. Tyler Duncan, otherwise known as Dust. He's a legend in our world, do I need to lay his accomplishments out for you, or have you heard of him?"

This time, it's Kid's turn to whistle. "Damn, I don't wanna know how you know him, but yeah, his reputa-tion proceeds him, I know all about him and his abilities. Continue," he says, rolling his hand at the wrist. If he wasn't the President of this club, and a founder's kid, with the attitude he's throwing my way today, I'd break the damn thing.

"Riptide Monroe, he's a mean son-of-a-bitch, and I personally would go out of my way to avoid him at all costs. The best interrogator this side of the Ho Chi Minh Trail. The things he comes up with to torture someone and get them to speak is unheard of and I'm sure illegal not only in the states, but worldwide.

Anyways, he has a one-hundred percent success rate at getting his enemies to talk."

"I've heard of him as well. Wasp and Tic talk about him all the time. They've said if he wasn't so uncontrollable and was manageable, they would've asked him to join years ago."

"He's definitely a man who walks to the own beat of his drum," I supply, "but I have a feeling we'll need him on our side."

"Who else?" I see him bent over, taking notes.

"Julius Walker," I'm interrupted by Ryder this time.

"*The* Julius Walker? Holy shit man, even if we don't use him, he's a man we need on our side," he says, tapping Kid's shoulder.

"Got it man, you've heard of 'em," Kid angrily responds. Something's definitely crawled up his ass since I saw him last.

"Andre Fortoney," I add, watching for their reaction to the name.

"The legendary assassin? No one has ever seen him, no one knows what he looks like, but you'r telling me you know him personally?" Ryder speaks up, with stars in his eyes.

"We grew up together, that's all I am willing to share about it. Other than the fact that he owes me a marker. And this is one I'm willing to call in."

"Do Wasp and Tic know you run in these circles?" Kid questions me.

"Of course, they do," I bark out. "I wouldn't hide shit like that."

"Just curious, brother. No need to bite my head off." I widen my eyes as I look at him. He's one to talk, he's been an ass to me since I first walked into his office.

"Sorry," he apologizes, running his fingers through his hair. "Got bad shit happenin' here and bad shit happenin' at home. Needless to say, my head is all types of fucked up." I nod my head in acceptance of his apology. I get it, happy wife happy life, unhappy wife and your life is fucked...or so I've heard. My wife is personally very happy, and extremely satisfied. "I'd consider it a personal favor if you could get them onboard with helpin' us out."

"Consider it a done deal," I say, standing up and exiting out the door. I really wanna go back upstairs and spend the rest of the day in bed with Lizzie, but I need to make these calls and see what I can do. I know these men will have my back no matter what, but can I get them all to agree and help the MC? That's another question that I don't have the answers to. But I'm gonna give it every-thing I've got to get them on the same page as I am.

———

I'VE SPENT THE LAST TWO HOURS ON THE PHONE negotiating. When I go long periods of times without talking with them, I forget how stone cold each one of these individuals are.

Jackson Ramero agreed right away. Anything that will get the blood flowing, he's down for. He could care less if he loses his life in the process. But usually, he's hunkered down behind his scope and rifle, so he doesn't get as much physical action as he'd prefer to.

Tyler Duncan, otherwise known as Dust, was a little harder to convince than Jackson. But he was nowhere near as difficult as Julius Walker was. I had to practically offer him my first born to get him to even hear me out. Once I laid it all out on the line for him, I had to promise we'd pay for all of his travel expenses, plus house him and feed him while he's here. That was the plan anyways, always was, but I didn't let him in on that knowledge.

Now, Andre Fortoney he's a different story all together. He's agreed to help, but from the shadows only. He won't be sitting in for any meetings, he won't be playing pinochle, his words not mine, and he won't be joining us for any Sunday socials…again, his words not mine.

I don't even know what a motherfucking Sunday social is! I think it's got something to do with ice cream and shit, but no one should quote me on that.

At least I've got some good news to take back to Kid.

Just another day at the office.

I'm hoping to convince these guys to join the MC. They would be a good asset to the club. Especially if they join Kid's chapter. They could really help him make a difference. We'll just have to see how things play out I suppose.

NINE

JUSTICE

ONCE I GAVE THE NEWS TO KID, I GRABBED A COUPLE OF beers and headed up to the bedroom to see what Lizzie was up to. I found her on her laptop, ordering some shit for our room. I tried to convince her we wouldn't be there long enough to enjoy it to which she replied, "It's still our temporary home, Justice. We need to make it feel like it." Not one to tell her no, I agreed, which is why I now find myself going over color choices of bedding and curtains.

"Lizzie, come on, baby. This is not my thing. I trust whatever you wanna do."

"Justice! This is our place, we need to make it feel like it."

"Beautiful, you'll be here more than me. Pick out what you like."

"So, if I get pink zebra stripes you won't give a care?" Now wait a minute, pink is definitely not my color. It doesn't show off my eyes.

"Okay, go with more blues and grey's, that would make me a happy man."

"Thank you, an honest answer."

"I never lie to ya," I begin to get upset.

"No, but sometimes you appease me, that's not what I want for us. I want us to be equals in this relationship. I want to make sure your opinions and thoughts matter as much as mine do."

"Damn you're sweet!"

"Not sweet, I just want to keep my man happy and satisfied. If you don't want to come home, then we'll never be happy together and make this work. And, Justice. I really want this to work," she implores.

"We will, we will work, Lizzie. You get me?"

"Yes, Justice," she smiles my way, "I get you."

"Good, now give me those lips." I command, leaning over the stupid computer that has become the bane of my existence. After she gives me my kisses, she leans back and studies me for a minute before she starts talking again.

"It's nearing dinner time. Are we eating with the club, or are we on our own tonight?"

"We're on our own, what are you in the mood for?"

"Pizza!" she says excitedly. Apparently, before we got together, she'd never had pizza. She's been testing out all different sorts. So far, the chicken alfredo is her favorite, but it's not something I enjoy too much. I am an old-fashioned type of guy, give me pepperoni and cheese any day.

"Do you wanna order and have it delivered, or go somewhere and eat?"

"Let's go out, I haven't been out of the club for a bit now. I'd like to see the city," she dreamily says.

"It's a town, babe, not a city."

"What's the difference?" Did she seriously just ask me that? Her parents did her no favors by only letting her be part of a certain few aspects of life. They've held her back, and where she appears naïve, and in a way is, she's also smart as fuck.

"Babe, a city has congestion, smog, bright lights, and no

one strolling the sidewalks. A town is full of stars, couples walking the streets, and not so many bright lights."

"Which do you prefer?" she curiously asks me.

"A town, babe. I like the smaller side of life."

"That's so surprising for me to hear."

"Ya, why's that?" I question her, curious about her answer.

"Because, you're so full of life!" she exclaims, like I should've known the answer and not asked her such a silly question.

"God you get to me," I state right before crushing my lips to hers. I show her with this gesture how much she's really come to mean to me. Our tongues touch, and I swear it's like a lightning bolt has zipped its way through my body.

"I don't know why I got such an amazing reward for speaking the truth. I wish I had your passion about life," she says this while looking me dead in the eyes.

"Baby, you are. You just need to find that one thing, other than me, that excites you."

"Ah, the only bad quality you have."

"And what's that?" I question her sanity. I have no bad qualities as far as I can tell.

"Sometimes, you're so full of yourself I wonder how your swelled head fits through doorways."

"You're going to pay for that remark," I voice, climbing on top of her and tickling her sides. My wife is very ticklish, and I appreciate it. Needless to say, our foreplay turns into another form of play and I go to dinner with my woman a very happy man indeed.

———

WE WALK, HAND IN HAND, INSIDE THE LOCAL PIZZA parlor. You can either order your own pizza, or eat at the buffet. We choose the buffet, so Lizzie can try different types of pizza slices.

"Ooh, Justice, look at that! Pineapple on pizza, who would've figured someone would use that as a topping?"

"A pussy," I answer, earning me an elbow to the ribs.

"Shhh, you could hurt someone's feelings. What if it happens to be their favorite?"

"Then they must have a pussy," I say, shrugging my shoulders.

"You just say whatever you think, don't you?"

"Yes, ma'am. Life's too short to beat around the bush."

"I wonder if I'll ever be that brave?"

"Hang around me and my family long enough, and it will come naturally to you," I humorously rib her. She enjoys it when I get playful with her, in our verbal sparring. I have the feeling she hasn't had too much of that in her short lifetime.

"I hope so," she says, paying attention to everything the buffet has to offer. I have a feeling I'll be standing in this line for at least an hour.

"I think I'm gonna try the pineapple and Canadian bacon pizza," she looks up at me skeptically.

"That's fine, babe. You have a pussy, so you can get away with it."

"You suck!" she whisper-hollers.

"Only on you, your skin, your pussy, your lips," I huskily respond.

"Only you have the capability of turning me on in a pizza joint, Justice. You and that wicked tongue of yours."

"As I recall, you appreciate this tongue of mine and what it can do to you."

"You're killing me here," she says, licking her lips as she steadily fills her plate. I doubt she is paying attention to what all she's piling on it.

"That's okay, I'll resuscitate you," I cheekily respond. I enjoy this flirting thing we do, I didn't do many things of this nature before she entered my life. It just wasn't worth it to me. No one piqued my interest enough to even try and be flirty. I was a hit it and quit it type of man, just living day to day and in my free time I would get my dick wet.

I know I sound like a real asshole, but it was my life. I didn't have to answer to anyone back then and I lived my life free and wild. And I enjoyed it at the time, I had no idea what I was missing. Now, I wouldn't go back to those days even if someone paid me to.

Finally, our plates are filled, and we look around to find an empty table. I don't like to sit in the middle, I feel like I'm too exposed. "There's one in the back, right corner," Lizzie points over to it. It's so dark over there that on my initial scan, I missed it. I must be losing my touch, looks like I need to stop only seeing my woman.

"Let's go," I say, placing my hand on her lower back and escorting her over there. Once we get settled, my back against the wall, I realize I like being non-descript like this. I can see the world around me, but I'm hidden, and no one will notice me unless I want them too. I watch in amazement as Lizzie eats one slice, then tries another. I can tell if she likes it or doesn't due to her facial expressions. If she likes it, her eyes widen and light up, if she doesn't like it, she scrunches her nose up and the lines in the middle of her eyebrows is dominant.

One of the things I appreciate most about her, is that you never have to guess anything. She'll either tell you, or you'll notice right away with her expressions. There's no second guessing, and no having to pry information from her. Now, I just need to help her be a little more comfortable in her skin, and help her build her self-esteem. When it's just the two of us, she doesn't hold back, and that's what she'll need to do with our family as well.

They'll respect her more for it in the long run.

TEN

LIZZIE

As soon as we got back from eating, Justice's phone rang. He looked at it, answered it and said, "Hang on a second," into the receiver. Then he turned and looked at me and said, "I really need to take this call, and I need privacy. I'm gonna step outside, love you." He quickly kissed me on the nose and strolled out the door. Without getting a replied 'love you too' back from me.

Instead of wallowing in my self-pity, I jump in the shower, brush my hair and teeth, then crawl into bed with my ereader. Since getting with Justice, I've been obsessed with reading the MC romance genre. Not that I expect this to be true-to-life, but it's exciting to see the author's spin on the motorcycle club world.

When I open it up and see the Author's Notes I burst out into laughter.

To my readers,

I want you all aware that this is a fictional romance book. This is my version of how they meet, fall in love and get their HEA…it means happily ever after… Real life versions of these men are not as I've described them. Please do not attempt to go out and search for your own biker. Most likely, since this is a make-believe world, you will not find what you are searching for.

If she only knew! I have that and more. I know that my reality is more like a fantasy, but there are really men like that out there…at least there is for me. I know there are some mean men and clubs, but I was lucky to get into the one I have. I've heard stories of death, destruction, and mayhem that is in our world. Hopefully, that never touches me or the ones I've come to care for, especially my Justice, but I'm a realist, and I know that something may one day happen to him.

For now, I'm going to live in my happy little bubble, and enjoy each day as it comes. I bury myself deep into the comforter, and put an extra pillow under my head to prop me up. I start to read, and when I get to a torture scene, I lay the book down. "They don't really do these things do they?" I question myself out loud.

"Do what?" I hear asked, causing me to jump due to being lost in my own thoughts.

"Nothing? Just something that I was reading in my new book I recently ordered. What are you up to?" I ask, breaking the ice and turning the conversation in a different direction.

"Have some paperwork in the lock box that I put in the closet. I need to grab it really quick to finish up my phone call. I promise, I shouldn't be much longer."

"No rush, Justice. I'm just laying here enjoying this book."

He goes into the closet then comes back out with a folder. I can see it jam packed with papers that look as if they're beginning to bend from being crammed into one single folder. Coming over to me he whispers in my ear, "You're gonna have to tell me more about this book that has you so enraptured." He nips my ear lobe, then saunters back out of the room.

I watch his backside, once again admiring the view.

Justice

"Got it," I express to Riptide as I walk out of the clubhouse and head over to one of the picnic benches. I grab my smokes, flick my lighter, and inhale. This is just what my lungs were begging for. I know it's not healthy, and Lizzie has recommended me quitting on several occasions, but that is easier said than done. When I'm stressed I could go through a pack and a half a day. That's thirty-five smokes.

Sometimes my lungs burn from smoking so many in a row, but I deal with it, and sometimes continue lighting another one. Just depends on the day and all I'm dealing with. My habit is what has kept many alive in my day. I've wanted to blow my top, but I'll pull out a cigarette and my mood changes, sometimes.

"Read me the report," he all but demands of me.

"Chill out, let me get situated." Everyone around me seems to be demanding shit from me instead of asking— nicely. Don't they know you can catch more flies with honey than with vinegar? Then I roll my eyes, because I highly doubt any of these guys have ever been nice in their lifetime. I get settled down, open the folder, and read him what I have so far on our new-found enemy. He grunts through some of the parts and whistles at others.

"That's a load of shit, brother. Can't wait to get my hands dirty, I'll be out on the next flight. I'll text you the landing information, pick me up personally." With that, he disconnects the call. Fuck, I still have four more calls to get through. I've already asked for help, now I need to give them all of the details. This is going to be one long evening. All I wanna do is get upstairs, crawl into bed, and enjoy my woman's body. There's no place better on this earth to be.

Looks like that may not be in the cards for me tonight after all.

Hours later—four to be exact, I finally make it to my room. The guys aren't usually so long-winded, but for some reason tonight, they were full of questions. Some of which I had answers to, and some of them I didn't. Which didn't particularly please them...at all.

I quietly slip into the bedroom, brush my teeth, and take off my clothes. I slide in under the sheets and pull my snoring woman into my arms. It's nice to know she's content enough, and feels safe enough, to fall asleep if I'm not here next to her. She's going to need to be able to do this in the next few weeks. I have a feeling I'll be gone more than I'll be here.

Which is fine, it's my job to protect the club and take out any threats.

I fall asleep, wrapped around her. Now this, this right here, this is what I'm talking about…paradise. That's how I feel when I'm with her.

————

I WAKE UP BRIGHT AND EARLY TO AN EMPTY BED. I HATE it when she leaves and doesn't wake me up first. I crawl out of bed and dress for the day. I walk down the stairs, and find her making two mugs of coffee. I nearly laugh when I see two bowls of cereal made and sitting on a tray. She doesn't cook, doesn't know how to according to her, but she helps wherever she can.

She burned noodles for macaroni and cheese the other night, so she was kindly escorted from the kitchen and asked to get a head count. Even though they didn't actually need one. They make enough food to feed an army, morning, noon, and night. They have to with how much this brood eats. "What'cha doin'?"

She jumps, and coffee splashes out of the mug and lands on her hand and wrist. "Fuck," she drops the mugs in the sink and I quickly make my way to her. I turn on the cold water and place her wrist under the faucet.

"Keep it there," I command her, "I'll go get the burn cream from behind the bar. Just don't move!" I say, walking out the door, looking over my shoulder to make sure she's doing as I told her to. She's still in the same position, so I hurry out of the door and walk into the common room and step behind the bar.

"What'cha doin' back there?" Ryder asks, coming over and leaning over the bar.

"Lizzie burned herself. I snuck up on her and she jumped causing her to slosh her coffee over the rim of her mug," I inform him.

"Damn, that woman of yours is a hazard to not only herself, but to food in the kitchen. May wanna keep her on a lock and chain to protect her."

"You aren't lyin'," I mumble under my breath. I grab the first aid kit and walk back into the kitchen. I grab a towel, and wipe away the drops of water from her skin.

"Ouch! That hurts," she says.

"I'm sure it does," I utter, blowing on it to help cool it. I pull out the burn cream and begin applying it.

"Shit! That's making it burn more!"

"Give it a chance to work, stop moving around like a jumpin' bean!" She's going to hurt herself worse than she already has if she doesn't stop jerking herself around.

"I can't help it," she whines. I take her arm and force it

133

still. I blow on it, but it seems to have the opposite affect than what I was going for. "No more, please just leave it alone," she begs with tears welling up in her eyes.

"Fine, no more cooking for you though. Stick to making toast and coffee. The other women will handle all of the cooking and coffee making from now on." She sticks her bottom lip out and says something I can't decipher. "Say that again?" I request.

"But I wanted to make something for my husband. It's my duty to care for all of your needs," she steadily pouts. But wasn't she just making coffee? Well, let's just nip the whole kitchen duties in the bud. I'd rather she not try to do anything that deals with heat. Ever. It's not safe for her or anyone around her.

"Then make me a bowl of cereal. I don't need anything fancy and shit. I'm a simple man with simple needs."

"You have a voracious appetite, I thought that meant outside of the bedroom too." She's too motherfuckin' cute.

"Oh baby, I do." I wiggle my eye brows causing her to giggle. "That's what I wanted to hear," I say to her, rubbing my thumb across her bottom lip. "There you go, all cleaned up and just as beautiful as ever."

"You and your golden tongue," she chuckles.

"I happen to know you worship this tongue of mine, golden and all."

"This is true," she agrees.

"Damn straight, now...what kind of cereal do they have here?" I stand up and walk over to the walk-in pantry and open the door. I start calling out all the different brands we've got and find my favorite. "Got mine, which one do you want?" I know she already had cereal made earlier, but it's some brand O'wheat something or other and ain't no way in hell that shit's going in my mouth. Riley must've left that shit sitting on the counter or something, she's the only one I know who eats that god awful shit around here.

"Let me look, some of the brands don't sound familiar to me," I move out of the way and start making my bowl. "They make cereal with marshmallows!" she exclaims, and once again I'm reminded of how deprived my Ol' lady really is.

"Yep, remind me to take you to the grocery store so you can see all the different types there are," I say, pouring milk into my bowl. "You want whole milk or that watered-down shit?"

"What's the difference?"

"I can see that we need a day of trying different foods

and drinks." I make a mental note to talk to the Ol' ladies and have them step in to help out with some of this. I don't want her embarrassed, but she needs to know there's more than a couple of choices out there for her.

"Sounds intriguing, I've never had a day of taste testing. Can we try some things out in the bedroom too?" She sounds so innocent asking this question, but at the same time it's seductive as fuck! Damn, I'm hard as a steel rod and if I didn't have to head out in thirty minutes I'd take her up to the bedroom and show her how to use some chocolate syrup.

"We'll need more than just a day for that adventure, beautiful."

"Yippee," she excitedly bounces on the balls of her feet and claps her hands. "Shit!" she exclaims, holding onto her injured one. "Guess I need to remember not to do that until I'm all healed up, huh?"

"Might be a wise idea," I joke with her.

"What are your plans for the day?" she inquires.

"I'm picking some buddies up from the airport. They're coming in at different times and on different airlines so I'm thinking it's going to take most of the day. What about you?"

"I'm going with Skylar, Sadie and Riley to get our nails and pedicures done. Then I think we're doing lunch and some window shopping."

"Do you know how to do that?" I tease.

"Yes, of course I do. But I can't help it, if I see something I like or want my wallet starts burning a hole in my purse. I can't allow that to happen, my purses cost as much as your boots."

"Your purses are a thousand damn dollars?" I don't know if I'm appalled or confused that women really have to spend that much on some bound leather that carries all of their junk.

"When they're on sale," she says, pouring milk into her own bowl.

"Are they fuckin' gold plated or some shit?"

"Nope, but most of them have registration numbers and tags."

"Like your motherfuckin' car?"

"Yep," she pops her 'p' dramatically.

"That's some crazy as fuck shit right there," I proclaim. I don't even want to know what her purses go for at top dollar. Women are fuckin' strange creatures.

Once I'm done scarfing down my food, I head to our room to get dressed. I grab my laptop to put into my saddlebag. I've got bikes being delivered to the airport for my friends coming in. While I'm waiting for each of them at the airport cafeteria, where they've all been informed to meet me at, I plan on doing some more extensive research on the fucking Ozzie Walkers.

I don't want any of this shit touching the club, but it looks like that's inevitable. I doubt the six of us will be able to handle this group of thugs on our own, but then again, these men have surprised me on multiple occasions. They're a force to be reckoned with on their own, but when they all join forces, the people of the world would be better off to go into hiding. They never give up and don't understand the words no or quit.

I kiss Lizzie bye and hit the road. This is going to be one motherfucking long ass day.

ELEVEN

LIZZIE

I'M LAID BACK IN THE CHAIR GETTING A BACK MASSAGE while the woman is working on my feet. This isn't as high-end as I'm used to, but it's a breath of fresh air and I'm loving spending time with the women. They are brash, and I find myself laughing at their antics and conversations.

I'm snapped out of my self-induced relaxation when Skylar asks me, "What color did you pick, Lizzie?"

I peel my eyes open and turn my head towards her and answer, "I'm going with the French tipped."

"That's so boring," she responds, rolling her eyes at me. "Live a little Lizzie, go for something more vibrant. Show the world you've joined the land of the living and are happy and unrestricted. Don't do what your parents would want you to do, do what makes you feel wild and liberated." I know she's trying to be encouraging, but I've never used neon or bright colors. My mother would have a panic attack if I'd have gone home with those kinds of colors.

"You know what? You're right, what color should I use?" I ask, biting on my bottom lip as uncertainty begins to take hold.

"Something fun and sassy," Riley states in excitement.

"What color would that be?" I'm unsure of what their definition is of sassy, but I'm sure it's much different than my own.

"Oooh, I know!" Sadie exclaims, "let me find you the perfect color! Please?" she begins to beg. I shrug my shoulders and nod my head thinking 'why not'? How bad could it be? She gets up and throws her sandals on, much to the lady who is working on her feet's dismay. A few minutes later she rushes up to me and shoves a bottle in my face.

"Absolutely not," I say shaking my head side to side. "Not happening, that color is hideous! Get it out of my face and try again," I demand crossing my arms over my chest. "There's no way in hell that…what color is that anyways?"

"It's a neon orange," she retorts while snorting her nose in my direction.

"That cannot possibly be an acceptable color, right?" I say, turning my head towards the other two. Skylar shrugs her shoulders and Riley is holding her hand over her mouth trying not to allow her laughter to escape.

"See! You've actually made them speechless. How often does that happen?"

"Hey, I sorta resent that," Skylar huffs.

"I have to agree with Lizzie, that's a god-awful color!" Riley admonishes.

"Fine! How about neon pink?"

"Pink sounds reasonable, I can do pink. Though normally I'd just go with a cotton candy pink. I'm not sure about neon, but I'll try it…this once," I say, holding my index finger up in the universal one-time show.

"We've gotta loosen you up, girl," Sadie says, stomping away in retreat. Hopefully to find a more appropriate color. I look down at my toes and send them a silent apology for what they're fixing to look like, promising them that we'll come next week and redo the color. I'll just wear tennis shoes, so no one sees that I've gone behind their backs and picked a color that's more me.

She comes back over with the brightest pink I've ever seen. Deciding it will have to do, I take the bottle from her and hand it over to my lady. "I'm going with that one," I tell her.

"You want flower?" she asks me. Thinking about it, I feel like it would add some character and not make it feel like such a bold statement. I need to take baby steps afterall.

"Yes, thank you very much." She nods her head at me and continues her filing. I have always taken meticulous care of my feet, so there isn't a lot she's having to do. I nearly crack up when I notice the cheese grater looking instrument come out by Skylar's lady. I look on in horror as she scraps that across the bottom of her heel and layer after layer of dead skin comes off. My mother started having my feet professionally done when I was in elementary school. She used to tell me how gross unkept feet are. I have a foot fetish to this day because of her and the words she'd use to describe a person's foot.

"I wear a lot of sandals and flip flops outside of the house. But when I'm home I'm barefoot all the way. It makes my skin dry. It doesn't hurt. You don't have to look at me as if it pains you."

"I've never seen that before, it looks like a torture device."

"It's not, I barely notice she's using it. What have you

been doing to get away without this ever having to be done to you?" she asks. Sadie and Riley look my way.

"My mother ordered us girls a foot mask. It lubricates and keeps the skin fresh and alive. I use it every night when I shower before bed. Then I put Vaseline on my feet and socks over that when they begin feeling or looking rough."

"You poor thing," Skylar says, shaking her head.

"Wait until you have kids, I promise you that will be a thing of the past. The only thing you'll care about is getting your body and hair washed. Oh, and when you shave your legs, it's usually during the summer. I am not as meticulous about it in the winter. I don't have time, I can barely keep my eyes open at the end of the day to complete my shower. Sometimes I hop in the bed soaking wet and crash before I realize I'm butt assed naked."

"That's because your children are demons," Sadie says as if she's informing her the sky is blue.

"They are not," Riley whisper-shouts.

"Honey, who the hell are you trying to fool? Your kids make me never want to have my own."

"That's your niece and nephew, Skylar!" Riley angrily states.

"Never said I didn't adore them, they just make me want to get a hysterectomy."

"I'm telling your brother," Riley pouts.

"Go ahead, he told Ryder the other day that they make his balls shrivel up and run away when he thinks of reproducing again. He gets it."

Riley's eyes drop down to her hands which are nervously twisting with one another. "I'm pregnant," she whispers, "he's not going to want this baby, is he?"

Sadie lovingly pats her sister's hand, "Of course he is. Skylar's just a bitch."

"I am," Skylar admits, eyes wide and she's bobbing her head up and down emphatically. "Don't listen to me, I'm just messing with you." She turns her head in my direction and widens her eyes at me. She's the one who stepped in this pile of shit all on her own, how the hell am I supposed to help get her out of this? I widen my eyes back at her and nod in Riley's direction.

"Fuck," she sighs under her breath. "Riley look, I just find it irresistible to yank your chain. Your kids are adorably sweet and so respectful. It makes me want to have a litter of my own."

Riley bursts out into uncontrollable laughter, "Now I know you're lying," she chokes out.

"And, here goes the hormonal roller coaster. All aboard," Sadie teases her sister.

"The crazy train is about to depart," Skylar plays along. We all end up rolling in giggles and unquestionably are eligible for the so-called crazy train Skylar mentioned.

We finish up our nails and go to lunch. Needless to say, I have an unforgettable time with these women. I'm getting to know a part of me that I had no idea existed. I'm ready to explore those pieces of myself that have been dormant all of my life.

Justice

I'VE BEEN SITTING AT THIS DAMN AIRPORT FOR WHAT feels like eternity. Both Riptide and Dust's flights were delayed. They were the whole reason I was up here as early as I was. There are storms where they're flying out of and I'm bored out of my ever-fucking mind. I've researched the Ozzie's until my eyes were ready to cross. Now I'm sitting here inhaling my fourth cup of coffee and my hands are shaky and my body is jittery with unrepressed energy. I have no way of expelling it so I try to keep my hands and feet as still as possible.

I don't have the intention of looking like some washed-up junkie that everyone can sit and stare at. I know I look peculiar sitting here for as long as I have, but honestly other people can kiss my inbred white ass. My dad did consider me a bastard so being inbred isn't too far off from that spectrum. I pull out my phone to give myself something to do when I feel someone come up behind me.

"Don't move motherfucker." My shoulders go slack when I realize it's one of my men.

"You son-of-a-bitch, Julius, you're lucky as fuck I didn't turn around and snap your damn neck," I playfully snap at him.

"I'd like to see you try," he snickers. I am not shitting you, he just snickered liked a god damned teenage girl.

"What the fuck ever, you know I could take you just like that," I tease, snapping my fingers together. The snap is loud, even to my own ears.

"Ooh, I'm shakin' in my snakeskin boots," he guffaws.

"Shut the fuck up, Romero, you motherfuckin' redneck asshole."

"Aww, now brother you may need to watch your words before you hurt my itty-bitty feelings here. I may need to shoot your ass if you keep it up."

"See, now you got me shakin' in my biker boots."

"I see you're still an asshole of epic proportions," he interjects.

"I've never claimed to be anything but," I reiterate.

"True 'nuff. I think we all are."

"That's one of the most honest things I've ever heard come out of your mouth," I inform him.

"Fucker, I never spout bullshit."

"You keep tellin' yourself whatever you need to so you're able to sleep at night," I tell him while packing up my stuff, so we have room at the table for both of us to be able to sit down.

We shoot the shit for the next hour and catch up. Finally, we're joined by Dust and Riptide. I know we won't be setting eyes on Fortoney, so we gather up luggage and head out to where I parked my bike. It's in an underground parking area and I'm happy to see the tow truck and our prospect, damn I've gotta learn their names, is already there with the extra bikes parked next to mine.

"Thanks, Probee," I say outta respect.

He nods his head showing respect back then states, "I'll be taking luggage back to the clubhouse so you gentlemen can enjoy your ride."

"Preciate it," Riptide says, slapping him on his back. I watch as the Probee is pushed forward and he takes a minute to get his feet to stand still. Once he's firmly on his feet, he has eyes wide open staring in my direction.

"You'll get used to him. He's a strong fucker who doesn't recognize his own strength."

He nods his head, then goes up to the men and gathers their luggage. "You're a good man," Walker says. Leave it to him to always try and smooth any waves that Riptide has caused. He's done it since our days in the service and since then every time we get together.

I wait as the guys debate over which bike is theirs. I roll my eyes in frustration because Riptide is a picky asshole when it comes to his ride. "Just grab a damn bike and let's roll!" I finally bellow out since my patience with their bickering has run out. I'm ready to ride and see my woman.

"Walker, stop being a dick and let me have that bike! The others are too small, and my knees will be up to my ears," Riptide states as he continues to ignore my statement.

"Might knock some damn sense into you if they bang you in the head enough." He goes for joking but Riptide looks like he's ready to fight. "Fine! You idiotic, stubborn tit bag, you can take the bigger bike. Whatever will shut you the hell up!" Riptide grunts at him causing a smile to spread across my face. Riptide isn't known to talk a lot unless it's something important to him.

"Now that you two have kissed and made up, can we get the hell outta here?"

The both nod at me so I fire my girl up. Once they've secured their helmets and started theirs, I lead them from the parking garage and head the long way home. After that encounter, I'm in much need of some road therapy.

Forty-five minutes later, we're getting ready to head into our territory when I hear some shots ring out. I look behind us in my side mirrors and see some low-riding Coupe Deville coming up behind Riptide. I call into our headsets, "You have guns in your left saddlebag, grab 'em and fire back!" I watch as they duck and weave while grabbing their pieces, I have a compartment that is in my seat where I hide my gun. I pull up the flap and pull out my trusty Ruger 9mm. She fits perfectly in my hidey hole, and I for one am ready to put some lead into these stupid kids playing at being grown-ups that have the balls to be firing at myself, and my friends.

These Ozzie fuckers need to go down, the sooner the better. I throttle my bike picking up speed so I can rush ahead of everyone. Once I'm far enough up the road, I turn around and head back going the wrong direction on the two-lane highway. I aim ahead of me as I travel towards my newly found enemy. Riptide and Walker spread out as Romero, Dust and I charge ahead. We are each firing our weapons. Ignoring the danger that I'm heading towards, my only thought is kill, maim and destroy.

A bullet whizzes past my head and now I'm livid. These fuckers are trying to split my head wide open like a god damned watermelon. I begin rapidly firing as my anger takes over. The five of us together are a force to be reckoned with. We can read each other's body language and know what the other is fixing to do before they do it.

Dust flies up ahead on the right side as Romero does the same on the left. This leaves me going dead center. Traveling at a high rate of speed, I lock onto the driver and aim towards him. I let my bullets fly making contact with my intended victim. I watch as his head slumps and the car veers to the right side, causing Dust to swerve. He manages to miss the car and turns around coming up from behind them. The car crashes into the guard rail and we surround it with guns pointed at all exit points.

Riptide puts down his kick stand and gets off his bike heading to the passenger front door. He whips it open and pulls the asshole out. He throws the kid on the ground and puts his boot over his throat. "That was a very stupid thing to do," he enlightens him.

"Fuck you," the kid wheezes out. "You'll all die!"

"Is that right?" I ask getting off of my bike and heading that way. "I think you've got your facts wrong," I advise him.

Walker walks around checking out the inside of the vehicle and whistles. "Looks like they're getting ready for the apocalypse."

Dust and Romero walk around and look in the back seat. They both whistle and look up at me. "You got 'em?" I ask Riptide.

"Yep, this little shit ain't going nowhere," he answers me. I'm satisfied that he's got this and walk over to look and see what it is they're seeing that has them all up in arms over. I look over at them to say something and see Dust is bleeding from his shoulder blade.

"That hurt?" I curiously ask since he hasn't said a damn word.

"I've had worse," he states, shrugging his shoulders.

"We'll have the town doc check it out when we get back." I walk over to my bike and get out my first aid kit. I pull out the gauze and the self-adhering bandage wrap

I have. I walk over and bandage his wound. Once I'm satisfied that it will hold until it gets looked at, I walk back over to the driver's side and pop the trunk. We open the trunk door and look inside.

"Holy fucking shit!" I murmur out. "I need to get Kid and Ryder here to see this shit. If this is what we're up against, we're in trouble." I pick up my phone and text Ryder giving him our location and asking him to come meet us to look at their supplies. "Kid and Ryder will be here in fifteen," I inform the guys.

"Need some cable ties to detain this fucker," Riptide hollers out. "I feel like the red-headed step child here being left out of all the fun." I roll my eyes and walk over to grab some rope and ties to secure him.

"Here, Rip, keep your gun trained on him while I bind him."

"My pleasure," he states.

TWELVE

JUSTICE

WE ARE BUSY ADMIRING ALL OF THE WEAPONS IN THE back seat and trunk as I hear multiple bikes pulling up around us. I recognize Kid's Harley right away and don't stress on who our visitors are. I hear Malibu mumble a 'fuck me' as he walks up to the side of the car. "What the fuck, were they planning to take out the entire town?"

"Not sure, man, but they are ready for some serious fighting," I reply. I introduce the men to each other, when they're done saying their 'nice to meet ya's', I then walk Kid over to the trunk. When he peers inside I see his shoulders stiffen.

"Need to get a van down here and pick these up," he says, pulling out his phone and sending out a message.

"We're going to confiscate these things and use their own weapons against them."

"Sounds like a solid plan," Ryder replies looking into the back seat. "They were out for blood today. No doubt about that."

"It's time to hit them where it hurts," Kid announces.

"Agreed," I answer back.

"Hell, to the yes," Riptide joins in on the conversation.

"That's what we're here for," Walker states, rubbing his hands together in glee.

"My sentiments exactly," Dust inputs.

"Then it's time to plan," Kid states. We stick around while the Probee that met us at the airport pulls up in the club's van. We all grab a handful of guns, launchers...etc. and load them up. It doesn't take long with us all helping out.

Ryder walks over to our tied-up compadre and kicks him in the ribs with a smile plastered on his face. "You, my friend, have a special place ready and waiting for your short stay with us." He walks away as the kid on the ground mutters all types of curses at us. We all laugh and continue on with our duties. When everything is put inside of the van, Ryder gets some duct tape and puts it across the asshole's mouth. "There, that'll shut you the fuck up." Riptide, Walker and Malibu pick up the jackass and toss him into the back of the van. I hear him grunt when he impacts and am happy that he had a little bit of pain inflicted upon him.

———

ON THE WAY BACK TO THE CLUB, WE DROPPED THE NEWLY acquired weapons at our warehouse downtown. It's monitored and secured by the local PD. Kid has made nice with the law enforcement and they appreciate that we've moved into town. Their crime rate has lowered substantially and it's because we've let it be known that there's a new sheriff in town—us, and we won't put up with, or deal with their bullshit. We run a clean town and will be judge, jury and executioner if they are caught by one of our brothers.

We pay a hefty fee to the police chief to make sure he has an incentive to stay on our good side. Chief Townsend has been a good asset to the club. He's stationed two of his top men on the property and is confident that they cannot be bought by the Ozzie's. They turned the other way when they saw our secured package in the back and even helped us offload the gun supply.

Rolling through the gates and pulling up to my parking spot, I notice the SUV the women took is still not here. As much as I wanna see Lizzie, this throws relief on me because I don't want her to witness us moving our hostage down to the basement. I know she's used to the sketchier side of life, but I don't want her to witness it from me this early on in our relationship…marriage.

I doubt that she'd bat an eyelash, but I'd like to ease her into some of our dealings. There's only so much as an Ol' lady she can be aware of, but there's no way you can hide an entire person. He's hauled down the stairs and secured in one of the cells we had installed. It's three o'clock in the afternoon and already feels as if I've worked twenty-four hours today.

I think back to the shootout, and am grateful that a shoulder wound was the worst of the injuries that was sustained. It could've been so much worse, it seems like someone was watching out for us. When things of this magnitude happen, I always feel like it's King watching out for his brothers from up above. He's always been protective of us and I'm ecstatic to realize that hasn't changed with his passing.

Kid reminds me a lot of his pops. He's a damn good President and learned so much from his dad. Ryder is like Sniper, his dad, was in the old days. Loyal to a fault and always thinking of the end game, it's what makes him the perfect VP to stand at Kid's side. Sniper had a mental break when he lost his best friend and President. I can't fault him for that, but I hate that he abandoned his club and brothers—not to mention his children.

Ryder, Kaci and Kassi pulled together and formed an unbreakable sibling bond. It reminds me of the one that Lizzie talks about when she refers to her sisters. I'm glad that they've maintained that throughout all of these years and the shit they had to deal with when it came to their father.

I go to my room and shower then change my clothes. I head out to the main room to see that my friends are getting along well with my brothers. I get a beer and sit down at the table and join them. I receive a notification and realize it's from Andre.

Andre: *While you were dealing with the pussies, I went and kept an eye on your woman and her friends. They're safe and headed your way now. I will continue to follow them until they are safely on the club grounds. You're welcome by the way.*

This throws relief on me, I did receive a message from her earlier that stated she was having fun with the girls and knew that she had a prospect on her so wasn't worried. But knowing that he had their backs, means that they have the best man on them that I could ask for.

Me: *Appreciate it. And I owe you one.*

Andre: *You owe me many.* This is a statement that I can't argue with, so I let it go and don't reply since I have nothing to add to the conversation.

Lizzie

I've had a blast with the women today. They taught me about being an Ol' lady and explained what was expected of me. Knowing that I can go to them with any questions makes me relax more with my new extended family. I was able to relax and be myself, something that I've never been able to express to anyone before now. When I told them that I am confused because I'm already in love with Justice and we haven't been together long, they all explained that it was the same way with them and their men. Insta-love isn't something I thought was possible, but apparently, I was wrong in my prior assessments.

As a matter of fact, I thought that it was a load of shit when I read about it in books. Who falls in love within a matter of days or weeks? It's a fairytale-fantasy that I find myself living in. I'm not saying that everything is perfect between Justice and myself, but it's as close to it as can be given the amount of time we've known each other.

I'm sure we'll go through some rough patches here and there, but I vowed to stand by his side through thick and thin and I won't go back on the promise that I made that day. I will prove myself to everyone that I'm trustworthy, and my loyalty is unbreakable. There was one woman, who I later found out was the President Wasp's Ol' lady, Ashton. She kept giving me odd looks during our wedding, reception and when we came back early from our honeymoon. I'm not sure what her problem is, but I'm used to people judging me before they get to know me as a person outside of my father and his organization.

I brush thoughts away of the scowling woman, and place my thoughts on my husband and new friends. I've felt judged by the men, but the women have accepted me with open arms. I need to build and concentrate on those relationships and hope the others will fall into place at a later time. Knowing that Sadie and Riley are this Ashton woman's daughters, I'm hoping that they'll convince their mother that I'm not a bad person.

I feel like I've got a personable personality, once people give me a chance, I'm easy to get along with…usually. Not always, I have had some female rivals throughout my lifetime. Mostly the girls who think they're too good for everyone else, but that's at every school and chick clique. I'm quite enjoying being included in this particular group. I've always had friends, but they were friends approved by my father. This always made me question if they were truly my friends or only because our families approved of each other.

As we pull up to the clubhouse and unload some of our purchases from some shops we visited, I am excited to see Justice. I know I've only been away for a few short hours, but I missed him desperately. I'm glad the girls can't read my thoughts and realize how needy I am in actuality. We walk through the door and the main room is filled to capacity, with some men and women I recognize and some I don't. As if Justice feels me enter the room, his head swivels my way and a smile graces his face. He gets up and walks up to me, he leans down and gives me a possessive kiss. I know he's marking me in front of the newcomers and I enjoy every second of it.

"Hey, beautiful. Did you have fun with the girls today?" he huskily asks me.

As soon as I catch my breath I respond with a, "Uh-huh." His smile widens as if he knows the kind of effect he has on me and my traitorous body. I could never get away with telling him I'm not interested. Every time he touches me my body reacts; my nipples harden and my pussy aches.

"C'mere, beautiful, and meet some of my buddies that I served with. They're goin' to be staying with us for a while." I look over and a big man, and when I say big I mean huge, winks in my direction. I stand tall with my shoulders back and head held high as to not show that he's intimidating me in the least. Justice grabs my hand and pulls me over towards the group he was sitting with when I arrived. "The man who's trying to be slick and flirt with ya is Riptide Monroe."

"How ya doing darlin'? It's nice to meet 'cha," he sticks out his hand. I reach forward to shake it showing my manners, he grabs my hand and turns it over laying a kiss upon the top.

"Keep your dirty mitts off my Ol' lady," Justice barks. Riptide throws his hands up in the air, but a troublesome smirk goes across his face. I can see this one here likes to make currents with his friends. "Moving on, this here is Jackson Romero, to his left is Julius Walker. These are men I'd trust the most with my life next to my brothers."

"It's nice to meet you all," I state, standing slightly behind Justice, not wanting any mishaps with these two.

"What are you doing with that loser?" the one he called Julius asks me. "You could do so much better than him."

"Fuck off, Walker! She's mine and she's not goin' anywhere...ever."

"Never," I reply to him, earning myself another panty-melting kiss.

"C'mon, let's sit and spend some time with the loser patrol." I laugh at his statement, because wouldn't that include him as well? I follow him like an obedient puppy and am anxious to get to know the men he served with. This is a part of him that I don't know, and would like to learn everything about him through their eyes and stories. The next few hours are spent with shots, beer and conversation. I find that I truly admire and like Justice's friends.

———

I MUST'VE FALLEN ASLEEP BECAUSE I AWAKE TO BEING carried up the stairs. "I can walk," I mumble.

"I've got you, sleep, beautiful." I lay my head on his shoulder and everything turns black. I trust him with everything within me, even in my sleep.

THIRTEEN

JUSTICE

I'm sitting in our meeting and my thoughts are not with my brothers. I keep thinking about last night and how well Lizzie got along with not only my brothers, but my team too. She had them cracking up, and they even joked with her that if she got tired of my ass they'd be waiting in the shadows to stake a claim. I normally would get pissed at that comment, but I decided to just go with the flow last night since she was eating it up.

"So, this is the plan," I take notice of what Kid says, and rejoin them in the present time. "Justice has already scouted their perimeter, we've got an idea of how they operate and their coming's and going's. We still don't know who their financial backer is, but we have a few ideas. Justice, do you have your notes to share?"

"Yeah," I pull out the folder that I had sitting in my lap and pass out the stapled packet with everything I've been able to find and see for myself. "In here is all of the information Kid has told you about and more. I have known associates from other states, and countries. They are small time, but with a big backer, which means they're fixing to grow by leaps and bounds if we don't put a stop to them. I have all the confidence in the world that we can end them before they grow in power and strength."

My men are in this meeting with us, we took a vote and agreed that if they're going to assist us, we need there to not be any secrets or unshared plans. Riptide is studying the paperwork as if it's a puzzle that needs to be solved. This is what he does, what he was specially trained for outside of interrogation.

"There's something missing," he mutters as he continuously scans.

"He's right, this is too much of a coincidence to have this many players in one field. Something's off, they're either playing these groups against each other, or these one-time enemies have joined forces, but my gut is telling me they don't know about one another," Walker adds.

"I'll get a hold of Cardozo and see what he knows. He

may want to meet in person, would you like me to set it up?" I question Kid.

"Yes, but include Ryder and me in that meeting, I don't want to get any information second-hand from this point on. I want to be in on any meetings or scouting that happens moving forward."

"You got it," I answer. He nods his head in acknowledgement. We continue on with the meeting and do some planning. We need more intel before we just jump in, this is where Cardozo and his men are going to come into play. I just hope bringing Lizzie's dad in on this isn't a mistake. I don't want my brothers owing my father-in-law a damn thing. I also don't want him to hold anything over my wife's head, like he's done to her for her entire life.

I won't allow him to continue to plague her life with his controlling ways. "You set up a meeting for as soon as possible, for now this meeting is adjourned but be ready at a moment's notice if we need to call another." Kid bangs his hand on the table dismissing us. Kid and Ryder stay in the room with Malibu. I walk out with the others and see Kassi, Kaci, Skylar, Sadie and my woman sitting around laughing.

I'm entranced by the breathtaking vision of her head

thrown back, her profile is just as exquisite as everything else about her is. When she tilts her head back down, she turns, and our eyes connect. She shyly smiles in my direction, and I briskly walk in her direction. I hear the whip sound from behind me and shoot the finger over my shoulder and keep moving forward towards my intended destination…my entire world.

"Hey, baby." Her voice comes out gruff and charms me straightaway. She's like a siren who's enchanted me to her. I lean down and kiss her, not caring who's witnessing my display of affection. "Love you," she sighs, causing bumps to develop on my skin.

"Love you too, my beautiful, sexy wife."

"There's that golden tongue again." When she says this all the women break down in laughter.

"Girl, we all know about that, don't we ladies?" Skylar asks the group.

"Sure do," Kaci affirms.

"Hmmm…these men know just want to say to get inside your panties," Kassi declares.

"Isn't that the damn truth," Sadie acknowledges.

"Whatever ladies, I've got a call to make, just wanted to

see my woman first." I lean down kissing her forehead. "See you in a bit." I start walking away, as I do I hear Skylar's smart-assed mouth running.

"See ya later, luv bug," I don't know how Ryder deals with her. She keeps him running in circles never knowing which direction is the correct one. He reminds me of a dog, always chasing his tail.

———

"CARDOZO," LIZZIE'S FATHER ANSWERS THE CALL.

"It's Justice, need to talk to you. Can we set up a meet?"

"If it isn't my wayward son-in-law, no pleasantries before we get down to business?"

"This is important, I don't have time for how are you's." This man gets on my fucking last nerve. I'm still sore at the things I've learned from Lizzie and his treatment of her.

"Fine, bring my daughter, her mother misses her. See you at five pm this evening, plan on staying for dinner." He disconnects the call. I hate being given orders by him and expected to follow like he's snapping his fingers and I'm to obey his every command. Fuck him! I'll give my woman the option and she can make the final decision on if she wants to come and sit at the same table as that asshole.

I walk in and search for Kid. He's still in the meeting room and the door is shut so I knock on it. "Kid, got a meeting set up with Cardozo," I announce.

"C'mon in," he hollers back. I walk in the door and see several rolls of blue prints laid out on the table. "These were dropped off at my place last night by the chief."

"What are they?" I inquire.

"Blue prints to their warehouses and compound," he answers my question.

"It's good to have friends in high places," I comment.

"That it is," Ryder agrees.

"Cardozo has agreed to meet tonight at five pm. He expects me and Lizzie to stay for dinner."

"Summoned by the in-laws?" Malibu inquires.

"Seems that way," I respond, "but it's ultimately up to Lizzie. I won't force her to be in their company if she doesn't want to."

"She's close to her mom and sisters, she'll wanna go," Kid reminds me.

"Unfortunately," I reply, "not really lookin' forward to sittin' across from him and pretending I like him."

"Maybe not, but we need him in this so do your best," Ryder states in amusement.

"I know we need him," I mutter under my breath. "Doesn't mean I'll like it."

"Understandable, but we all do what we gotta do for the club," Kid proclaims.

"I didn't say I wouldn't do it, guys. But you all owe me one, or twenty."

Lizzie

JUSTICE HAS BEEN BEHIND CLOSED DOORS FOR A WHILE now. I decide to run upstairs and jump into the shower. When I get to my room, I see my phone on the night-stand and realize it's lit up. I walk over and swipe the screen to see what notification I have received.

Father: *Your young man needs a meeting tonight. We expect the two of you to join us for dinner. Your mother and sisters miss you.*

I sigh, I miss my mother and sisters, but having to deal

with him is not my top priority. But, if that's the only way I can peacefully visit my family, I'll do what I have to do. I take a deep breath and reply to his text message.

Me: *I will be there, father.*

I know I have to take my father with a grain of salt. Now, I need to mentally prepare myself to deal with him and pray that Justice doesn't leap across the table and strangle him to death. I've only shared tid-bits with Justice about my childhood.

I fear for my family if he is to learn about the basement and how it was used to put me in my place when I disobeyed or spoke out of turn. He knows that I was a foreign concept in my home. My opinions and feelings didn't matter...still don't, and that I was controlled in every aspect of my life.

The things he doesn't know as of yet, need to stay as far away from him as possible. One, I don't want him looking at me with any pity. Two, I want him to get to know my mother and sisters without the judgement of them sitting back and not standing up for me. He'd never understand why they couldn't.

He won't understand that they did help me in the only ways they knew how without becoming the brunt of my father's punishments. Just because they didn't get as much punishment as I did, doesn't mean they weren't under the lens of his microscope as much as I was.

It was just different, their punishments weren't the same as mine, Father was always imaginative when it came to showing his displeasure in us. He knew that I couldn't handle solitude, which is why the basement became my form of torture.

The more creative he was, the happier he became. I don't know why he hates us as much as he does, but he at least pretends we matter in the public eye. We always looked forward to having company, it's the only time we felt human—wanted. Our family dynamics are so much different from those I've witnessed here, but it's all I've ever known. I need to take notice of how everyone here works, and try to insert that bond into mine and Justice's relationship. I don't want him to ever feel left out, or wishing he had what everyone else does.

I hop in the shower, I shave, wash and condition my hair and exfoliate my face and skin. I'm not sure how long I've been in here for, but when I get out, dry off and wrap a towel around my hair and one that's fastened around my chest. I'm not paying attention to the bedroom as I walk over to the closet to look for what I'm going to wear this evening.

"I take it you've heard from one of your parents?" I jump and scream.

"Shit, you scared the ever-loving crud out of me," I state, with my hand over my chest.

"Is that right?" he snickers. "Crud, are we getting prepared for no cussing already?"

"I guess so, I didn't even realize I was doing it. You know how my parents feel about inappropriate language, especially at the dinner table."

"You do know your father cusses like a sailor, right?"

"Never in the house, at least not in front of us or our mother," I state as I shrug my shoulders.

"What would happen to one of you if you were to slip?"

"I'm not sure about now that we're grown and married, but none of us have ever felt courageous enough to try and see what would happen, Justice. But, you be yourself, I like you just the way you are, and my family will just have to deal."

"That's good, because I won't change anything about myself for anyone. Ever. So, it's a damn good thing you like me just the way I am."

"I love you, Justice. I enjoy your filthy mouth, your devotion, shit, I appreciate everything about you. You wouldn't be the man I've fallen in love with if not. Keep doing you, and who cares what anyone else thinks. Judgmental people can kiss our asses. We just need to keep being ourselves and if someone else can't stand beside us, understand us, or not want to talk their shit about us, that's on them and something they'll be called out on eventually."

"You sound like you've had practice," I can hear the curiosity in his tone.

"I know when you were in school you witnessed the mean girls club?"

"Sure, I saw how catty bitches can be."

"Exactly," I state nonchalantly.

"Does it ever get better for you women the older you get?"

"It can, depends on someone's maturity level and if they're willing to not follow a leader and have a mind and thoughts of their own."

"Followers are pussies, it's crazy to not like someone because someone else doesn't. That's childish and they need to go back to kindergarten and relearn respect and manners."

"Some don't have backbones and have to hide behind

others. I actually feel sorry for them, it means they have no self-esteem and weren't taught to appreciate themselves."

"You're too good, beautiful. I don't see hair pulling in your future."

"You'd be surprised what I'm capable of. Especially if I'm pushed into a corner. I may look naïve and skittish. But I have been known to scratch an eye out."

"I've seen a feisty side of you," he teases me.

"I can be feisty outside of the bedroom, don't doubt my mad skills, Justice."

"Never," he says, getting up and walking over to me where I've stayed stationary by the bedroom closet as we've had this conversation.

"Good," I whisper as he closes in on me.

"Give me those lips, beautiful. I've gotta get in the shower and shave and shit."

"Literally shit, or other things you need to do?" I inquire, don't ask me why I wanna know this. I couldn't honestly answer that question.

"Shit, shower, shave...same routine as always. Lips." I lift up on the tip of my toes and pucker out my lips. He pulls the towel off of my head and throws it on the ground. He grabs a hold of the back of my neck and fists my hair. He's talented that way. "Lips," he growls as he leans down and slams his down on mine. When he pulls back, I'm breathless. "I'm not dressing up in somethin' stupid," he avows as he walks towards the bathroom door.

"Yourself, Justice. Just be yourself...I personally prefer the tight jeans that snug your luscious ass." He wiggles his hips at me before he shuts the door.

I like it when my man is in a playful mood.

FOURTEEN

LIZZIE

As we head towards my parents' house, I bite the inside of my cheek. I know I should be excited, especially getting to see my sisters, but I'm always hesitant when it comes to being in the same place as my father. I sound like a broken record, even to myself, but I can't help the things that go through my mind.

I feel Justice as he places his hand on my knee as we're stopped at a stop light. He gently taps it letting me know he feels my tension. I'm not trying to upset him in any way, shape or form, but I can't help the tightness of my body and chest. I place my head between his shoulder blades and squeeze his waist. Kid, Ryder and Malibu are with us which makes me feel better. I know they'll be able to hold Justice back if Father pisses him off. At the same time, I grasp that they will not be there at dinner and it will all lay on my shoulders to keep him feeling balanced and in control of his emotions.

We arrive all too soon and my nerves are jumping, and my hands are clammy. Did I make the wrong decision agreeing to do this? It's too late now to change my mind I suppose, unless I feign illness. For some reason, I don't think that would fly with the guys nor my family. There has to be a reason that Justice's brothers are here. I just hope my father isn't too much involved in whatever it is. I trust him as much as a catfish should trust a worm on a hook—not one bit.

The front door opens as Justice assists me off the back of his bike. I see my sisters standing in the doorway with grins spread across their faces. They are pushing each other aside as they begin to charge my way walking briskly because we were trained that women don't run or rush anywhere. It's funny how they make a swift walk look so elegant and choreographed.

"Izzy," Genny hollers in excitement. She's always been the more exuberant one. Rosa is more quiet and reserved, but I can tell that she's just as happy as our sister is to see me. I'm wrapped in a huddle of hugs and am filled with their tenderness. They've always been able to do this for me whenever I've been filled to the brim with anxiety. "Father's in his office, take a deep breath, baby sister." I do just that and pull back looking at my sisters. They both look just as happy and bubbly with life as I feel.

"Marriage looks good on you," Rosa tells me.

"That's because I have the best husband in the world," I say, sticking my hand out for Justice to grab.

"It's because she's easy to love," he replies taking my outstretched hand in his. I gasp, because it's the first time he's used the 'L' word in front of anyone…especially his brothers, at least none that stands out. He's shown me in so many ways that this is how he's felt, but I never thought he'd voice those thoughts out loud. My heart is rapidly beating in my chest, only this time it's for a completely different reason than it was on the ride here.

My sisters' faces light up at his declaration and I know we're going to be having a womanly conversation about my relationship. I can't wait to share everything with them. I trust no one more than I do them…but that's quickly changing.

Justice

I'M LED INTO CARDOZO'S OFFICE BY HIS BUTLER. IT FEELS

as if I've entered the world of some sitcom. Who the fuck is so lazy that they need someone to answer their god damned door? I bet they have a maid and cook too. This errand boy knocks on the door and informs him that his visitors have arrived. I could've done that shit, I don't need someone to announce my arrival. My voice and hand works perfectly fine.

"Come in, gentlemen," he states, standing up from his chair. The desk he has between us is massive in size and I don't understand why someone needs something so ginormous. Is he trying to compensate for something that's small? Just an observation, I'm sure his wife is unsatisfied if he has to have bigger things surrounding him.

"Cardozo," Kid says, sticking his hand out. He reciprocates the gesture and shakes his hand. "It's good to see you again," now I know he's lying out his teeth because he loathes him.

"Same, please sit." He directs us to some chairs in front of his desk which he sits down at once again. I watch as he pulls up his slacks and crosses one leg over the other one. "What can I do for you this evening?" he casually asks, plucking the end off of, then lighting up a cigar. I'd bet you dollars to donuts it's an expensive Cuban he's fixing to be puffing on.

Kid and Ryder take the seats, but I lean on the door. I casually cross my ankles and my arms across my chest. I'm hoping this meeting will be quick and dinner even faster. "We need to know what you may know about a group of misfits that have moved into our territory. They call themselves the Ozzie's, but their true name is…"

"I know who they are," he interrupts Kid. I notice that his shoulders stiffen and I'm waiting for him to teach this motherfucking father-in-law of mine some manners. "What information is it you're in need of?"

Kid clears his throat and continues, "We have intel that they have several financial backers. Would you happen to know about any of these groups or corporations?" He pulls the file out of his cut and slides it across the desk.

He opens it up and a chuckle escapes him. "Marsalis organization wouldn't be happy to hear about the fact that they are being played by this group of 'misfits' as you call them. Neither would the Jiménez's or the Arcola's. You may do well putting a bug in their ears if you get my meaning."

"Would you happen to know someone who could get the word out to them?" Ryder inquires.

"I have several who wouldn't mind seeing their displeasure," he opens a drawer and grabs a phone out of it. He places it on the table then says, "it's you're call, would you like me to get the ball rolling in your court for you?"

"We would appreciate that," Kid acknowledges.

"I'll need proof, may I make copies of these?" he asks, holding the folder up for us to see.

"That is a copy, you can keep those. What about these others?"

"These others, I could start a war and end these miscreants without you having to lift a finger. They'd squash them like the annoying pest that they are." I look at Kid hoping he won't agree to this, I would personally like to put my hands on several of these jackasses, especially the ones who knew and agreed to the shootout that involved me and my men.

"We would be willing to have the assistance from them if they're willing to speak with us personally, we'll set somethin' up with them."

"They do not work well underneath others, but I'll see what I can do to help out my daughter's new family. Anything else I can aid with?"

"If you could pass along this number," Ryder says, passing the club's business card across to him, "we'd be grateful."

"Your club willing to give me a marker for sticking my neck out like this?"

"We would, unless it's somethin' that will blow back on our club or get one of our Ol' ladies hurt."

"This now includes your daughter." This is the first interjection into the conversation I've made.

"I would never do anything to harm my daughter. It would devastate her mother," I didn't hear anything about how he'd feel in that declaration. I'm not sure how to take that, it also makes me want to have a one-on-one conversation with him. I'm not sure how productive that would be, but I'd like to use him as my personal punching bag. "Dinner should be ready any moment now, you boys are welcome to join us if it would please you," he indicates Kid and Ryder's way.

"Thank you for the offer, but my wife and children are waitin' for me at home," Kid politely declines his offer.

"Some other time then?" I can't tell if he's for real or living in some fantasy land, there's no way in hell either Kid or Ryder would sit down at a meal with him.

"Well see," Kid says as I move away from the front of the door and open it. I let them out first, but don't show the same for Cardozo. I walk behind Kid and Ryder having their backs and placing Lizzie's father at mine.

Yes, it's a sign of disrespect, but he has a long way to go to earn any from me.

———

After my brothers leave, I'm shown to the fanciest living room I've ever seen or stepped foot in. I can't believe people actually purchase gold statues and shitty ass artwork. Give me some dogs playing poker and I'm a happy man. I could splash some paint on a canvas and sell it for a million more than what I spend on supplies. And, it'd look ten times better than this sore spot my eyes are currently trained on. It's like a mack truck, you know it's coming, but you can't seem to get the fuck outta the way of its path.

"Justice," Lizzie whispers catching my attention.

"What?" I question her.

"What are you lost in thought about?"

"That," I point at the picture, "is god awful, why the fuck would someone pay for that? I could do the same thing for half the price...fuck that, a quarter of the price."

"Don't let my mother hear you, that's her pride and joy. She went all the way to Paris to an art gallery to purchase that particular piece. She even stayed with it all the way home to make sure the transporters didn't trade it for a fake or not treat it like a piece of glass as it was moved from one plane to another."

"Lizzie, please tell me you will not put something so atrocious in our home."

"Nope, I don't really care for it personally. Plus, I see you as more of a dog playing poker type of man than that."

"Thank you! I was thinkin' the same thing not too long ago. Those dogs make me laugh, who wants staleness in their house instead of it filled with fun. I want someplace I can come home and relax in, not somethin' I have to avoid to preserve it and keep in pristine condition."

"Like the clubhouse?" I hope she's kidding, but I can't tell.

"Well," I say, scratching the back of my neck. "Not exactly, something relaxed like it maybe, but more homey."

"Homey?"

"Can we have this conversation later when your entire family isn't staring at me like I'm some sorta science experiment?"

"They are not looking at you in any such way."

"Really? Cause I sure do feel like a bug under a microscope right about now."

"Dinner is served," some woman comes in and announces.

"Thank God," I blow a breath out of my nose. "Let's get this done and over with," I say, grabbing her hand and following the woman's lead.

When we get to the 'formal dining area' I'm more nervous to sit at the table than I was to sit my ass on their fancy couch. "You have got to be kidding me," I utter.

"What?"

"Are we even allowed to sit on those chairs without puttin' down a deposit?"

"Don't be silly, Justice. Here, sit next to me," she says pointing at a chair. I watch as her father pulls out her mother's seat and decide I can at least be that much of a gentleman, so I copy his moves.

"Thank you," Lizzie says as I pull out her chair, wait for her to sit and push it in. Only, I do it with a little more force than necessary and I see her head bob from the impact.

"Sorry," I tell her as I take my seat next to her. She grabs my hand under the table and laces our fingers together.

"No worries, Justice. Remember what you promised me? Just be yourself."

Myself. Right, I can do that.

FIFTEEN

JUSTICE

I can't do this! I'm going to leap over this table and punch that motherfucker right in the jaw if he has one more jab to make towards my Ol' lady. So far, her clothes are inappropriate for dinner, she's gained weight and her teeth aren't as white as they used to be. I was waiting for him to state before she married me, but it never left his big fat trap.

Swear to God, I'm tasting blood in my mouth from how hard I've bitten my tongue. Lizzie pats my knee which calms me a little, but not much.

And then the bashing continues, "Why is your face so made-up? You look like an overzealous clown. Ladies do not wear so much," she waves her hands around in my

Ol' ladies' direction, "junk, and still be expected to be perceived as a lady," her mother states.

"That's it, I've had it! There is nothin' wrong with her clothes, makeup, weight or anything else you are tryin' to find fault in. Not a *God damned* thing! She's beautiful, intelligent and so full of life that she brings that to others surrounding her. People gravitate towards her, they appreciate everything about her as do I. I will not sit here and let you demean and belittle her. She's mine, from now on if you have any problems where it concerns her, you come to me!" I holler, pointing at my own chest. "I can't and won't in good conscience allow you to make her feel like there's anything wrong with her, because to me she is perfection."

I look at my Ol' lady and see tears rolling down her cheeks and it angers me even further. "See what the fuck you assholes did? No one makes my wife cry. Not one motherfuckin' person, not even me."

"I'm not crying because of their cruel words, Justice… I'm used to them. I've heard the same song and dance all of my life. The reason behind these tears is because of your beautiful words and declaration. No one has ever stuck up for me when it comes to my parents," she sniffles.

Her mom has a smile hidden behind her glass as she has

it at her lips pretending to take a drink. Her sisters, Genny and Rosa, aren't hiding their smiles, however, and their husbands are shifting uncomfortably in their seats. Cardoza on the other hand is studiously inspecting me. I scowl back at him and stare him down letting him know in my own way that he doesn't faze me in the least and I can give back to him as well as he can give to me.

"Shall we go ahead and finish our dinner in peace and leave Lizzie alone?" he finally states with a sneer across his face. Lizzie's mother nods her head in acceptance and everyone's eyes go directly to their plates. The men continue eating, while the girls spread their food around on their plates while still smirking at their father being put in his place, at least that's what I'm assuming it is from.

As I eat, I continuously keep my eyes on everyone else to make sure they understand and comprehend that I'm keeping an eagle eye on them. One wrong move, one wrong word, and my hands will be firmly wrapped around their necks. End of story.

———

"Well, that was…fun," Lizzie says as we crawl into bed later that night.

"Fun isn't the word I'd use for it."

"Keep on growling, Justice. You know what that does to me," she states, rubbing her hand across her breasts.

"Oh yeah," I purposely growl out again...just to see how far she's willing to go. She moves her hand down over her night shirt and slips it beneath her panties.

"Again," she begs. What the ever-loving fuck! This shit is a wet dream come true. One of her hands is furiously moving beneath the fabric of her panties while the other one comes up and starts plucking her nipples over the t-shirt...my shirt that I insist on her wearing to bed. I don't usually like her wearing panties, if I want her or need her in the middle of the night, my pussy needs to be accessible for my dick to plunge into.

"Strip, Lizzie...show me what's mine. I wanna see my pussy and my tits."

She stops her ministrations, and looks up at me like I've grown horns on the top of my scalp. She methodically gets up on her knees and slowly removes her top. She takes her fingers and circles her buds. I lick my lips and rub my dick over my jeans which are growing tighter by the second. My cock is feeling strangled and I swear I can feel every tooth on my zipper. She hooks her fingers in the sides of her panties but doesn't move. She sits there staring at me. Challenge accepted...wife.

"You wanna play this game? I'm in," I state as I prowl

towards my prey and lean over her, causing her to rear back and her back bends to make room for me to invade her space. "I hope you don't like this particular pair too much." I take my knife out of my pocket and use the space between her fingers and skin and tear my blade through the fabric, first the right side then the left. She gasps, but I know it's not in fear as her chest begins to heave and her breathing becomes erratic.

"That's so sexy," she purrs. Well, if she liked that, she's going to enjoy this even more. I put my hands on her shoulders and push her to where she loses her balance and lands on her back on the bed. After a few bounces, she stills, and I admire the view in front of me. Her hair is fanned out over the mattress and pillow. Her head is nestled in the crook of where they meet. As she begins to rub her legs together, I remove my clothing.

"Spread your legs wide Lizzie and play with that beautiful pink pussy of mine." When we first got together, if I gave her these commands her face would turn beet red in embarrassment. The more sexually active we've become, the more adventurous she's gotten.

When her finger hits her clit, she moans out my name, "Justice." This spurs me into action, my dick is ready to plunge inside of her wet, tight sheath. "Please, I need you buried inside of me. I'm aching all over," she slurs.

"I'll get you there. Patience, beautiful." I crawl over the bed, placing my thighs between her spread legs. My eyes laser onto her fingers as they circle, invade, and exuberantly play with her sweet pussy. Having had enough, I pull her fingers away and see the glistening that layers her lips. I pull them to mine and place them in my mouth. I suck all of her juices off and moan in delight at her tangy flavor as my buds explode from the essence.

"Fuck," she groans. My head goes between her shoulder and neck as I breath in her scent. She has this unique fragrance about her, it's vanilla and strawberries combined. No one else displays the same aroma as she does, and it makes me feel like I'm home. I've never been attached to a certain smell, but something about her's draws me in like a moth to the flame. She puts her hand between us and grabs my hard as fuck dick. She strokes it several times as my hips shift in her hand and slide between her fist. She lines me up to her entrance and lines my cock head to her opening. I thrust forward until my balls slap her ass.

"Fuck, Lizzie. You're so tight, it's like I'm taking your virginity over and over again every time I enter you. Fuck you feel so damn good," I utter into the crook of her neck.

"It's because you're so big," she pants out. "Move, Justice, please. I need to feel the force of the combination that is you and me. Take me—hard, let me feel every inch of you." Her mixed words between proper and sexual frustration are my ultimate undoing. I pull out and slam back inside. "Yes!" I begin to pound in and out of her.

"Fucking hell," I pant out as I try to breath between her squeezing the life out of my dick and the effort it takes to get back inside. Her channel is already clamping down on me with every forward thrust. "Not yet, baby. Don't come yet, we've just gotten started."

"It's hard," she implies.

"You've got this," I pull out of her and turn her over by grabbing a hold of her ankles and twisting. Her body follows, and I take a pillow from the head of the bed and position it under her hips. It raises her up to the angle I desire and I slam back home. My fist grabs a hold of her hair and I hold on for a wild ride.

"Oh fuck, you're so much bigger this way," she cries out. I swivel my hips to make sure I hit her sweet spot. "I'm gonna come!"

"Not. Yet," I bark out. She reaches under us and grabs my balls in her hand. She begins to lightly squeeze and roll them. My eyes roll in the back of my head as I lose control and come inside of her calling out her name. My release sets hers off and before I know it, we're sprawled out on the bed trying to catch our bearings. "So damn good," I manage to get the words out.

"Every time," she proclaims. I get up and go to the bathroom to grab a wet rag to clean us up. Once that chore is done, I crawl back into bed and pull her into the crook of my arm. We both fall blissfully asleep wrapped in each other.

Lizzie

I WAKE BRIGHT AND EARLY THE NEXT MORNING WITH THE sun shining on my face. I stretch my arms out and notice that the place beside me is empty. Rolling over in disappointment I smile when I see a note resting on his pillow.

Lizzie,

You were so peacefully sleeping that I didn't wanna wake you. I had to go out today and take care of club business. You rest, relax, and have a calm day. Last night will be ingrained in my thoughts the entirety of the day.

See ya soon, beautiful,

~Justice

HE CLAIMS HE DOESN'T HAVE A SWEET BONE IN HIS BODY, but he proves that it's a lie every time he opens his mouth. He'd get all growly and call me a liar if I was to call him out on this, so I just shrug my shoulders and secretly jump for joy inside. I only see him this way with me and it makes me melt inside to know he loves me as much as he does.

I think back to the way he took up for me with my parents and comprehend that I need to start doing that for myself and not depend on him to do it for me with everybody. I lay in bed and ponder this for a few minutes. I want to be strong, liberated, and never allow anyone to walk all over me again. I want to be respected by his brothers and him to be thrilled to have me on his arm, just as the other men are with their women.

I internally giggle because I know that Justice would shit his pants and have a conniption fit if I became anything like Skylar. Justice claims that Ryder needs to get a leash to keep up with her and make sure she stays where she's supposed to. She is always on the go, but she's so damn self-reliant and doesn't care or worry about if Ryder is going to approve of what she's up to.

She's so much damn fun to be around, that I usually

forget to behave the way I've been trained to do. She and the girls make me strive to be free and content with who I am, not who they expect me to be. With a new plan in place, I set off to get ready to face a new day. One where I don't ask for anyone's counsel or guidance. One where I spread my wings and be the true me. I've come to the conclusion that I don't need to try and become a new me, I just need to let the girl loose who's been buried inside of me for all of these years, begging to be set free.

"You will never again self-discriminate against yourself," I tell myself as I look at myself in the bedroom mirror. "You are a good and captivating person, show everyone who you really are."

SIXTEEN

JUSTICE

I woke up early to my phone going off. It was a text from Kid stating that he heard from Cardozo, and he set us up a meeting first thing this morning with the key players we were asking him to speak with on our behalf. I didn't wake up my sleeping beauty because she looked so serene in slumber. Instead, I left her a note and dressed, leaving her for the day.

"Cardozo told me that Dominique Arcola, and his bodyguard are tremendously interested in speaking with us," Kid informs me. "He also confirmed that Cesar Marsalis and Raydon Jiménez are insistent that they are allowed in on this meeting."

"This should be fun," I retort.

"A day at the circus sounds like more fun to me," Ryder speaks out. Have I mentioned that Ryder has been terrified of clowns since he was a small child and went through a funhouse and one grabbed a hold of him from behind? He's never been able to go to the circus or look at Halloween costumes without having a total freak-out.

"I'd pay a thousand dollars to see you go," I declare in a joking manner.

"You can go fuck yourself, Justice."

"Nah, it's not as fun as fuckin' my Ol' lady," I retort.

"I'm gonna tell her you said that," he teases.

"Go ahead, she appreciates my dick," I emphasize this by grabbing my package.

"Y'all stop fuckin' around, we've got business to attend to," Kid scolds us. And just like that, we turn around and head out the doors towards our bikes. Heading back to the house of terrors that I was at the previous night. I know I made some waves with my in-laws, but I don't give a shit and will walk into that house like I own the damn place.

They will learn I'm not a man to be trifled with. I may not be in an outlaw club, but we don't take any shit either. We've lived and learned from our past mistakes...

ones that I will not be making with my woman. She will be protected at all times, if not by me then by one of my brothers or prospects. If her family can't get on board and help me out with this, then they need to learn to stand back and let me control her safety and happiness. A job I will take very seriously.

WE GET OFF OUR BIKES ONCE WE SHUT THEM OFF IN HIS driveway. I see three limos with men guarding them. I take off my helmet and place it on my seat. I turn and walk to the door and instead of waiting for the butler fucker to answer, I turn the door knob and walk right on in. I see my mother-in-law sitting in the front room. She looks at me with a warning, but I only give her a head nod and continue walking down the hallway.

I can hear Kid, Ryder, and Malibu's boots pounding behind me and ignore any protest they may be making. I understand them not wanting me to start any shit…but hell, I'm family now. No need to be announced or let in, right? Stands to reason from my personal view. I do, however, knock on Cardozo's office door, not willing to push my luck too far past the point of redemption. It's a respect thing not to walk into someone's office space… especially when there may be something confidential. I know I didn't show this level of respect walking into their home, but I had a point to make and I think I made it effectively.

"Enter," I hear called and open the door and walk in, holding it open for the guys. "I hear you made my home yours," he asks me with his face pinched.

"Thought we were family," I raise my eyebrow with the statement.

"We are, but please wait to be announced next time." Whatever...maybe. We'll see what sorta mood I'm in when next time comes. I look him dead in the eye but do not verbalize a response. "Gentlemen, please have a seat and let me introduce you to my guests."

After introductions, we get down to business. I've made enough copies for each one of them to have their own. Needless to say, they aren't happy with being played by the Ozzies. When they realize that our territory has been breached they are once again, extremely displeased. There's a code in our world, one that shouldn't be compromised unless you're willing, and ready for a war to break out.

Dominique Arcola is the first one to speak out. "I am very displeased with the actions they've taken. I didn't sanction any such actions and I most certainly didn't give my consent for them to invade your territory. We've never had an issue with the Rage Ryders in the past and don't wish to have one in the future."

"I have to agree with Dominique," Cesar Marsalis states. "We want no beef with your club. We are just as much victims of them as you are. We will stand beside you and help you rid yourselves of these vermin."

"Same with my family," Raydon Jiménez states. "We weren't aware that they'd be using other backers and suppliers, or we would've never agreed to work with them in the first place. We have our own territories that we've given them permission to work from, there was no need for them to come into yours."

"Then we're agreed this issue needs to be resolved, immediately?" Kid questions them.

"Yes."

"Absolutely."

"Whenever you're ready to strike."

"You will also have the Cardozo organization as an alliance. We are ready and willing to work with our new family." I'm sure they are, and I can't help the huff that comes out of me. I know this is the whole reason for mine and Lizzie's arranged marriage, but now I know her, I love her and I'm not happy about the way she was used as a bargaining chip by her father.

He looks at me and I can see his displeased look. Not that I give a fuck, but Kid smacks me on the back of my shoulder. This time, I look away from my father-in-law and ignore his looks and snide comments. I just want this meeting done and over with.

They plan on getting more information for themselves and we have another meeting arranged with the families in one week's time. When we do come together next, it will be to plan our attack on those Ozzie motherfucking Walkers. Numbers were exchanged, and I briskly walk out of the house and sit on my bike waiting for my brothers to be done.

I couldn't breathe in that house, in their company any longer. I had to escape, I needed to catch my bearings and clear my thoughts before I speak with Kid or even Ryder again. "You alright?" Malibu asks as he walks up next to me and lights up a smoke.

"Let me have one of those," I demand.

"Thought you quit years ago?"

"I did, but it looks like some old habits have a way of coming back and biting you in the ass."

"You having a hard time dealin' with her family?"

"You have no idea, brother," I inform him. Her father may not be physically abusive, but he's bringing up a lot of old wounds that I thought had already healed. And watching her mom reminds me so much of my own, they are both meek and selfish. Neither caring or wanting to save their children from the monsters they married…it's all about them and what they are or aren't willing to put up with. Who cares if it jeopardizes your child's safety and emotional welfare?

"You ever need to talk, I'm here," he says.

"Same," I respond, knowing that he and Kassi have had a rough go of things since Fern was murdered. Each one of them dealing with it in their own way. It's a push and pull relationship with them. One day they can't keep their hands off of each other, and the next they're making each other miserable. I can see the devastation in my brother's eyes whenever he thinks about Fern.

"I'm doin' alright, brother."

"Just in case, I'm here."

"Appreciate ya."

Kid and Ryder come out the door and walk over to us. "You alright?"

"I'm good," I respond to Kid's question.

"Then let's get the fuck out of the Addam's family home. They creep me the fuck out." I bend over laughing at his observation of the Cardozo's. He couldn't get any closer to the truth than he just did. Addam's family...I'll have to remember to use that when describing them.

Lizzie

SOME OF MY PACKAGES ARRIVED TODAY SO I BEGIN making over our space. The bedspread is soft, but not feminine. It's a dove grey with a rug and sheets to match. I wanted something smooth on my skin, but not something that would blind Justice and make him never want to crawl into this bed with me. I got some black accent pillows, lamps, and wall décor. One decoration I like the most is a metal hanging display of a motorcycle. I think Justice will appreciate the fact that I thought of him when purchasing things for our room.

No one was around when the package was delivered that I recognized. So, when the prospect brought them to me, I had him carry them up the stairs and place them in here. I'm now standing here, hands on my hips, trying to devise a plan to get these things hung up. I've got the bed made, the tables on the nightstands and I know where I want each piece hung up at, but I'm too damn short to reach. I look at the hammer and nails I threw on the ground and want to pick them up and throw them in frustration.

I wanted everything done so I could surprise Justice when he returned. I leave the room and stomp down the stairs, looking for someone, anyone to help me. Still seeing no one in the main room, I then decide to head into the media room. And when I enter, I blush from head to toe. Jackson, Dust, Riptide and Julius are all watching a porno. I've never seen one before and am embarrassed to be in the same space as one that's playing out on the television.

I'm baffled when I see a man shove his fist up some poor woman's va-jay-jay and before I realize I am doing so, I ask the men, "Is that really possible? This is fake...please tell me this is photoshopped or some shit."

Riptide roars in laughter while Julius looks at me and winks. "You've never heard of fisting?"

"Is that what that's called?" I ask, pointing at the tv.

"Yep, you should have Justice try it some time, you may enjoy it."

"I do not think so," I exaggerate, and draw out each individual word. "I don't think mine could even stretch out that far," I advise them.

Riptide moans and grabs his dick. "Darlin' don't suggest how tight your pussy is to men who are watching pornography and have no women around to take care of their needs. It's impolite," he enlightens me.

"From what I understand from the single men here, there's a strip club downtown that caters to all sort of needs, maybe you should check them out."

"Are you informing me that I need to go and hire a whore? Darlin' I don't pay for services, women beg me to let them get a piece of all this," he drags his hands down his chest before cupping his manhood.

"More information than what I'm needing to know," I come back.

"That's more than any of us needs to know," Jackson inputs. "Now, was there something you needed, Lizzie?"

"Oh, um…yes, I have some things I need hung up and I can't reach."

"Wall hangings?" he asks me.

"Yes," I answer.

"Well, then you need a man with muscles, I'm your man...show me what you need."

"Thank you, Jackson."

"Now wait a minute, I got muscles," Riptide bellows from behind us since we already started walking down the hallway to head up the stairs.

"We aren't talking about the muscles in your lower head," Jackson teases provoking him.

"At least mine's something worth talking about," Riptide clowns back.

"You keep telling yourself that, brother." I decide to ignore the knuckleheads and keep moving in hopes that they'll shut up and follow my lead. Which they do, thankfully.

———

WHEN EVERYTHING IS ON THE WALLS, I FEEL AS IF I should pat myself on the back for a job well done. Justice is going to be happy with all of this. It's nothing like my parents' house, but has a little bit of each one of us shown.

I rush around and make sure all of the boxes are broken

down and grab them under my arm pit, ready to carry them down the stairs and put in the dumpster out back. As I walk through the clubhouse and out the back doors, everything around me explodes in gunfire. I hear shot after shot as I drop the boxes and run behind the building looking for a good hiding spot where I won't get hit.

I've never been curious about how a gunshot wound would feel, and I'm not going to start wondering now. As I rush around the back, I see two young men jumping the fence, I nearly stop thinking they're here to help until I notice automatic weapons in each one of their hands. I look around frantically trying to figure out how to hide with the least amount of exposure…from both the men and guns.

As I rush around the building, I see a little vent on the bottom part of the clubhouse. I am thankful that I still have the mini flathead screwdriver in my pocket from putting together some things earlier. I start to unscrew them and when I get all four of them loose enough to pull out, I grab the panel and yank with all of my might. It flies over my head, but I don't care if it's in plain sight or not.

I slide my arms above me and use them to pull my weight inside. Just as my waist breaches the seal, I feel my ankles grabbed and my body pulled back. I grab onto the sides and try to pull against my would-be attackers. I will be no one's victim! I begin screaming and kicking my feet, but whoever it is that has a hold of me has a firm grip and I'm struggling to get loose.

"Looks like I've got myself a feisty one, Marco," I hear a young male voice imply.

"I'll never let you take me!" I holler as I try to pull myself back through the hole.

"Keep struggling, I like a good tussle." This statement fuels the fire within me and causes me to fight just that much harder. I finally manage to get my right foot free and start kicking anywhere I can. I can't see them since my vision is blocked by the outer wall, but I'm not going to stop until I hurt him in any way I can.

I hear a group of motorcycles and know in my soul that it's my man and he will rescue me, and fucking put these wanna be gangsters six-feet under where they can never scare, hurt, or take anyone against their will.

"Justice!" I begin screaming with all of my might. Continuously screaming his name, my throat begins to feel raw and abused, but I don't stop, I keep yelling not caring in the least about the damage I'm most likely inflicting upon myself. The struggle continues on for what feels like forever before I feel the hands on me let go and I'm shoved into the underground pit that is pitch black and I can't see anything in front of me.

I hear a scuffle outside, but I don't try to see what's happening, instead I find the deepest and darkest corner I can make myself invisible in and hide like the coward I am.

SEVENTEEN

JUSTICE

WHEN WE PULL UP TO THE COMPOUND I IMMEDIATELY know something isn't right. Brothers are running around outside, fights have broken out and I become frantic knowing that I left Lizzie here while all hell has broken loose. My fighting instincts kick in and I slam my kick-stand down right here inside of the gate and rush the grounds. I throw my helmet on the ground, not even caring if I crack it beyond repair.

I rush to help Dust as he's fighting off three men. He's holding his own, but I mean come on, three against one is a little spineless on their end. I notice one asshole pull a knife and run after him. The other two are keeping his attention while the other one comes in for the kill. They've got the whole conquer and divide thing down, but I'm fixing to put an end to that scenario.

I grab him by the back of his head and slam him forward. He loses his footing and falls head first onto the ground. I jump on his back and push his face into the unforgiving dirt. His body jerks since he's not able to get any oxygen in his lungs. I lift my face up and notice my brothers holding their own. His body stops struggling and I jump up and off of him when I hear my named screamed out in fear. I'd know that voice anywhere, I start to follow it until I make it to the back of the building.

I can hear the whiz of bullets as they fly around the air. A few fly pasts me, and I feel the wind from the speed of the bullets as they leave the chamber of the guns. I duck and weave, and somehow, I miraculously escape getting hit. As I make my way around the building I see legs sticking out of the basement crawl space and realize I know those legs. They belong to *my* woman!

And there's not only one, but two fucking boys, who have the gall to place their hands on my property. They are dead men walking! No one puts their hands on my woman and lives to tell about it...*no one*! Seeing nothing but them, I run as fast as my legs will let me and tackle the one whose hands are around her ankles.

"I'd suggest you get your motherfuckin' paws off my woman!" I roar, letting my anger flow through my words. I take my left hand and shove her through the opening before turning and depositing my concentration back on the thugs. I am looking forward to putting a beat down on these thugs. "I'll gladly give you a head start if you're too scared to face me now." I express this, because one of them has his eyes darting around looking for an escape route, and the other one looks like it's taking all of his mental focus not to piss his pants.

I would laugh, but they had their meaty paws where they didn't belong. That's not acceptable in any way, but in my world, it's a sentence for death. "Aww, you gonna play with both of 'em? I'm left unsatisfied. Let me give you a helping hand," Jackson casually strolls up next to us saying.

"Fine, but I get that one," I disclose, pointing to the punk who was holding my woman back from escaping the danger that he was part of placing her in. My body begins to quiver, my anger spiking, and my adrenaline is pumping through my veins.

Ignoring the pathetic whimpers that leave my intended victim's mouth, I rush him needing to get this out of my system. My right hand draws back in a fist and I slam it as hard as I can making contact with his nose. I see the blood squirt which does nothing but fuel my desire to witness more coat his body. I let my left hand fly, and it connects with his ribs.

Again, and again, I switch back and forth slamming my fist on his body wherever it lands. His hands are in a defensive position as he tries to block me from making contact. I'm needing him to fight back, I don't want a punching bag, I want a quarrel. "Fight me back, you pussy!" I spit the saliva from my mouth, trying to make a statement.

"I'm sorry," he whimpers in agony. I've gotten in a few kidney shots, so I know he's in pain.

"You're motherfuckin' sorry! You're a pathetic waste of space! Get up off the ground and fight me like a man. What's the matter, you were all gung-ho on fighting a woman, but you can't face me like a man?" I antagonize him further. "Did you lose your dick somewhere between grasping my woman against her will, and me taking that play toy away from you?"

"Fuck you!" he hollers out, exhibiting the first sign that he has some balls buried in there somewhere.

"You may be a man after all," I sneer. I'm an asshole, sue me. I rush him, and he bounces up on his feet, taking a fighter's stance. Who does this asshole think he is, Muhamad Ali? I'm not a professional fighter, I fight dirty. After I was shot and went through extensive physical therapy, I've learned to take my punches where I can and cause the most damage feasible. We end up charging each other, blows are exchanged, and I black out. I don't recognize or realize the punches I'm receiving—my mind is blank.

Lizzie

I CAN HEAR A SCUFFLE, GRUNTS, AND I RECOGNIZE MY man's voice. I want to go back up and help him fight, but I know I'll be more of a hindrance and distraction to him, than actually helping. I dig myself further into my hiding space and bury my head in my hands and cover my ears. My eyes are squeezed tightly shut so I am not tempted to look around my surroundings. It's dark, damp, and I'm scared of what may be living down here. I hum a tune that I remember from my childhood that used to ease and calm my nerves.

You are my sunshine, my only sunshine...

I sing the tune in my head repeatedly, trying to erase what's happening above ground. The question keeps playing on repeat in my mind, 'Is Justice safe? Has he been hurt?' My worry is making it harder to stay here where I know I'm currently safe. The need to be by his side is overwhelming my good intentions. I get up from my spot, and walk towards the light. It's the only visible thing down in this hole. My eyes squint the closer I get. The sun is blinding compared to the darkness I've been in.

'You've got this, Lizzie,' I state to myself in my mind. He would do it for me, what kind of Ol' lady am I if I don't at least check on him? This is what I keep voicing to my conscience every time it rears its ugly head and tells me to stay the fuck away and wait for Justice to come for me. I should've listened to the angel on my left shoulder and ignored the devil positioned on my right. He's a convincing son-of-a-bitch.

I must get too close to the window, because before I realize what is even happening, someone reaches in and pulls me out. A cloth goes over my nose and mouth causing my eyes to water and my nose to sting. My last thoughts before the lights go out is telling Justice how sorry I am for my impromptu need to put myself in a situation that wasn't my place to do. 'Please forgive me, Justice,' I shout out in my head.

————

When I come to, I panic with the darkness that envelops me. I slow my breathing, trying to get my brain to slow down and think. I have no injuries, other than this hammering headache. It's dark, but I feel movement beneath me. Think…what's the last thing you remember? It's bleak, nothing standing out, zilch is coming to me scarce of feeling my heartbeat inside of my skull. It's rapid and painful. I'm having a hard time catching my breath, but I cannot understand why…panic attack?

What the hell did I get myself into? I close my eyeballs, I take a lung full of oxygen and add up to three, then let it out. I implement this deed until I feel my heartbeat condense in tempo and my head, although it still hurts, isn't so manifested.

My lids open wide when I realize… 'Holy fuck, I've joined the Ol' ladies kidnap club!' Justice is going to go ballistic when he gathers his thoughts and takes notice of the fact that I'm not where I should be—waiting for him to grab me when he feels it's safe to do so. I have a feeling that when he finds me and brings me home, my ass is going to be so raw I won't be able to sit for a month.

For some odd reason, I'm not scared. Well, at least not from my kidnappers. I know that if Justice and the Rage Ryders don't find me quickly, my father and his organization will. I don't know which one of them I wish to rescue me, they both will be hard to deal with when it happens. I just wonder whose wrath is going to be worse? Justice will be pissed, but my father's had more practice with punishing me and knows what to do to get me to break quickly.

Damnit, I've just become a statistic. Huh, guess I really will fit in with the rest of the women. We'll have a lot to talk about on the holidays…comparing kidnapping and rescue stories. Oh, and which of our Ol' men are more creative with their punishments. I have a feeling that no one will be able to top mine, because he's protective and possessive when it comes to me and my safety.

I subconsciously rub my ass when I imagine already feeling his hand print there—and he hasn't even found me yet. I come out of my inner deliberations when we hit a bumpy road and I'm bounced around like a rag doll. Jesus! I push my hands upwards and push on the trunk, trying to brace myself when it pops open suddenly. Not much, just a sliver, so I quickly act by placing one of my hands in the opening, preventing it from hitting another bump and closing.

It smashes on my hand several times and I bite back the curses that want to be voiced out loud. My other hand has grabbed a bar on top to keep it from bumping too far up and taking a chance of the driver noticing it. I straighten my legs out, trying to secure myself since my hands are needed for other things.

My head bounces up harshly and I slam it back down on the unforgiving trunk's floor. I see white spots, making my already sore head more so. I end up biting my tongue and can taste the metallic flavor that floods my mouth. It makes me gag, but I work hard not to vomit from the amount I have accidently swallowed.

My ears hone in on a conversation consisting of murmured voices and I comprehend that I have more than one captor. I utter a quick prayer to a God that I stopped believing in a lifetime ago that I can manage to get myself out of this circumstance on my own. Hopefully, that will help Justice and my father go easy on me. It may be wishful thinking, but that's where I'm currently at.

"I've gotta take a piss," one of my captors says to the other one.

"You can't wait twenty fucking minutes?" I hear the other one ask.

"Only if you want me to take a piss in your car." This is what I need, they'll be distracted, and I can make my escape.

"No way, fucker, I'd be forcing you to lap that shit up

with your tongue. Fine, I'll pull over, I'll drain the snake while you are."

"What about the girl?"

"What about her? She'll be out for at least another hour and she's secured in the trunk. Let's go before I change my mind." I hear two car doors open and shut in succession. I place my ear near the opening of the trunk and listen to hear their footsteps, trying to decipher which direction they're heading. It sounds as if it's towards my head, so I quietly lift the lid, and crawl out. I don't stand, I stay low to the ground. I gently close the trunk and hear the latch click in place. I duck walk the other direction until I get to the side of the vehicle. Seeing the woods all around me, no matter which way I look, I make the decision to sprint as fast as my legs will allow me, and keep running until I reach or find, some sort of civilization.

I'm not sure how long I've been doing this, but my legs are screaming out in protest. I am so out of shape, I make a mental note to join a gym and build my stamina. I never look back, I don't stop for odd noises, I just keep moving forward.

The more time that passes by, the darker it's becoming, and I realize I'm lost. I don't know if I've been going in circles, or if I'm actually making any progress. My body is shutting down and there's no way I can keep moving. I find a large tree surrounded by brush. It has to be the best place I can rest. I'll be out of sight, and I'll be able to close my eyes…for a little bit. I know I can't be here long, but I have to give my body the respite it's in dire need of.

EIGHTEEN

JUSTICE

WHEN I FINALLY FINISH WHIPPING THIS ASSHOLE'S ASS, I observe that he's no longer breathing and there's no movement from his chest. I won't waste my time checking his pulse. Satisfied that I gave him the *justice,* - no pun intended, - he deserved, I go and squat down by the opening and call out Lizzie's name.

"Lizzie, baby? It's safe to come out now." It's silent, the hair on the back of my neck stands on end. "Lizzie!"

"Think she fell asleep down there? She could've had an adrenaline crash," Julius says, walking up behind me.

"Maybe, anyone got a flashlight so I can go down and check on her?"

"I do," Riptide states, squatting down next to me and removing the one he carries from his utility belt.

"Thanks, brother," I take it from him. I turn it on and place the end between my teeth. I take my hands and grab ahold of the seal. I use my legs and push myself inside. My hands land first in the dirt floor, I wrap my large hand around the base of the light and hold tight as I pull my legs through. I go through faster than antici-pated and my knees slam into the unforgiving ground. I bite back all the fuck you's that go through my head and instead I lift up. I can't stand on my feet down here, I'm too tall, so instead I crawl around on my recently damaged and already swollen knees. Are they sore? Sure, but my brain is on a mission...find our woman.

"Lizzie, baby, can you hear me?" I call out. Still, silence surrounds me, and an overwhelming sense of dread wraps around me. Squeezing my chest and stealing my breath. Something's wrong.

"Justice, brother, we've got a problem," Kid shouts out.

"What? I'm a little busy down here," I scream back.

"You're not gonna find her down there, brother," he hesitantly states.

"What the fuck is that supposed to mean?" I query.

"That's the thing, we checked the feeds and saw two

men carry her out. She was unconscious, brother. We've got a direction to follow. The plates are being run and the two that survived the attack are down in the cells. If we can't track her on our own, we'll get the information from them."

"We're not waiting!" I bellow. "Kid, while I'm out searching for her, I need someone in there interrogating those fuckers!" I demand as I crawl back out.

"Fine, we'll head out and Malibu…"

He doesn't get to finish that thought before Riptide interrupts him. "I'll do it, it's what you brought me in to do anyways. Go find your woman, while you're searching, I'll get everything I can from those pieces of shit." He puts his hand out helping me stand.

My body is hurting from fighting, and being cramped down there, so I thankfully accept his extended hand. I hear, and feel my bones creak and pop, as I ease my legs into a standing position. I'm getting too motherfucking old for this shit. "Let's go," I command, ignoring my achy body and rush for my bike. I don't even check my helmet that was tossed to the ground, I ignore everything other than hitting the road and finding my Ol' lady…my heart, my soul, my world.

"Which way?" I request.

"East," Ryder responds.

I ask no further questions as I start my bike and head out the open compound gates. I don't look to see if anyone is following me, because I know that they are. I do not do a damn thing other than look for a vehicle that's out of place, looks like it's speeding to get away. I didn't ask about the vehicle's make or model, I just hauled ass...I just...just *want*, to find her.

My missing link.

My joy.

My forever.

Ryder and Kid pass me by and I follow since they do know the information I'm lacking. What was I thinking? I know better than to leave without all the pieces to the puzzle.

I only had tunnel vision.

Seek.

Find.

Destroy.

Revenge overtaking my mind—pain. Slaughter. Death.

As soon as Lizzie's safe and sound in my arms, that's exactly what I'll be doling out.

———

We did nothing but run in circles, never finding the sedan that Kid and Ryder were searching for. I've never been so fearful of anything or for anyone in my entire lifetime…not even my mother when my father was teaching her a lesson. I stomp into the clubhouse, my current mission is to find out what Riptide was able to pull from those two pussies.

"He's in the interrogation room," Ryder informs me as he catches up with me. We walk side-by-side down the hallway. When we hit the stairs that are behind a locked door, he pulls out the key and waves his hand in front of him indicating that I should go first. I don't acknowledge this gesture, I just take it and jog down the stairs.

I hear Riptide laughing and it pisses me off. This is not the time for games and jokes. When I hit the bottom of the stairs, I nearly throw up at what I see. "Is that…is that his dick?" Ryder asks me, his face suddenly a dark shade of green.

"If you can't handle it, get the fuck out! He has answers and we need to get my sister back." Riptide announces, and if it was a better time, my feet might've been dancing at his declaration of my woman being like a sister to him.

"I'm good. Continue," Ryder pronounces, one hand waving air in his face while the other one is holding his throat. "Fuck that's sick," he says, turning around looking at the wall. I nearly join him, but I can't seem to take my vision away from the man Riptide is currently torturing answers from. "He's got some serious issues," Ryder mutters under his breath. If he only knew, I've seen much worse than someone's dick being cut off and shoved up their own ass. I don't even want to imagine what his compadres may be doing to my woman.

An hour, and many missing parts later…he tells us where they planned to take her. We all run out of the club-house, not caring about the man we left in tattered pieces below and haul ass to the location he indicated.

"Please, Lizzie," I start begging I'm not sure who.

Please be there and alright.

I refuse to live this life without you, baby girl.

Lizzie

I WAKE UP, MY BODY SHIVERING. I DON'T KNOW IF IT'S from the nightly chill in the air, or if it's because my body is crashing from the excitement and adrenaline of the day. I try to stand, but my feet are asleep, and I cry out as the sharp, needle-like pains that run from them extend up my legs. I must've been in this position for a quit awhile if that's happening.

I'm not sure if it's safe to leave my hiding spot or not, but I can't stay here forever hoping and praying that someone I know, and trust will find me. I have to take this in my own hands and make certain that I make it back home safely to my family...to Justice.

My teeth begin to chatter, and I notice that my shirt is torn. I'm not sure when it happened, but it's not giving me any protection from the night's chilly air. I rub my hands up and down my arms trying to create some friction. It starts to work, but then my hands become like ice, pain slicing through them.

Knowing I won't become any warmer standing still, I begin walking the way I was before I needed to stop for a break. I walk and walk for what seems like forever before I find a dirt road. Instead of traveling down it, I decide to stick to the shadows and hide behind the trees and follow the trail. I'm worried that if I show myself, those who took me could find me and snatch me again. Just because I haven't seen, or heard anyone, doesn't mean there's not someone out there looking for me. Hunting for me. I refuse to be anyone's trophy prize. I wouldn't look good hung above some maniac's mantle.

I'm suddenly thankful that it's night time, because the road is lit up from the moonlight. "A full moon," I whisper to myself. "Not sure if that's a good sign on a night like this or not," I continue to mutter, talking to myself.

I'm exhausted, I'm not sure how much longer my legs will hold my body up. I just want to sleep, but it's so cold that I'm not sure I would be able to accomplish it. Long-ingness hits me and the desire is strongly evident that I'd prefer to be snugly wrapped in Justice's arms, on my nice, fluffy bed, and comfortable sheets and comforter. I would break down and cry if I wasn't worried that the tears would freeze to my face.

"Ugh…how long had we been driving for anyways before I woke up?" I wail in anguish. "This could only happen to me. I don't wanna be part of the kidnap club anymore. I don't give a damn about holiday conversations, or bonding over our men and experiences. Why me?" I scream out. "I'm not a bad person, I've never hurt anyone. Am I being punished for the sins of my father? The weakness of my mother? The freedom I've finally found? The love I've finally felt? It's not fair!"

I hit my knees and begin to make promises of what I'll

do if '*He*' sends Justice to me. "What have I ever done to you? You're supposed to be all powerful and merciful, care to show me some?" I don't listen for an answer, knowing that I won't be getting one. Looks like I'm on my own.

Is this some sort of test? If so, I admit I've failed miserably. Giving up, I lay down right there in plain sight, not caring who finds me or what they do with me. I'll cross that bridge when it comes. For now, I just need to lay here and wallow in my agony.

While I'm laying here, freezing my tail end off, I contemplate my life. Not too long ago, Justice and I said our forever's and promised to always be there for each other. I can't help but wonder if I'll be the one who breaks those vows and promises. As the chill wracks my body, I have a hard time holding on to consciousness. I feel myself sinking into the darkness.

My imagination is playing tricks on me, because I swear I hear a band of motorcycles coming up the dirt road. I listen harder, and realize I'm not dreaming at all. No one will find me in this field, I force myself to get up. Only every time I get on my feet I collapse.

They're going to pass me by and never realize it. The third time my body gives way and I land on the dirt, I conclude the fact that we all had to crawl before we walked. So I do it old school, I crawl. I feel branches and sticks as they dig into my palms and knees, but don't let that deter me from my objective.

I must seek help.

I will not survive another ten minutes in these elements.

As I reach the road, I look up to see if I recognize the cuts on the bikers. When I do, and know it's them, I find what little strength my body has and stand. I run out in the middle and wave my hands like a lunatic.

Bikes begin to slow down. One nearly drops to the ground as the rider comes barreling towards me. My legs shake, I call out, "Justice!" before gravity once again takes hold. I fall to the ground, only this time it's to shouts of my name.

NINETEEN

JUSTICE

Kɪʟʟ. Sᴇᴇᴋ. Dᴇsᴛʀᴏʏ, ɪs sᴛɪʟʟ ʀᴜᴍʙʟɪɴɢ ᴛʜʀᴏᴜɢʜ ᴍʏ mind as we take the back road towards their hideout. I'm not one-hundred percent positive that I'll find Lizzie there, but I won't give up until I have her wrapped tightly in the embrace of my arms. We're twenty minutes from reaching our intended targets when I see something come out in the middle of the road. It takes me a minute to comprehend that it's not a wounded animal, but the woman I love.

My bikes skids to a stop when I hit the brakes and I make it off the bike and am running before the kick stand completely settles on the ground. I'm running, calling her name and my heart skips a beat or two when she collapses to the ground. "Noooo!" I scream out in agony. I couldn't have just spotted her to losing her in as little as three minutes…tops.

"Lizzie!" I yell at the same exact moment in time that she hollers out my name. I see her eyes roll into the back of her head as her body makes contact with the earth's floor. I make it to her and scoop her up into my arms.

My brothers surround me, and I can hear Kid shouting out orders. "We need a bus here a-s-motherfuckin-p!" Riptide, Julius and Dust are all looking at Lizzie as if they've lost their best-friend. No! She's okay, she'll be fine…she has to be. I stroke her hair as Julius checks her pulse. I look up at him with begging eyes, he nods at me letting me know her pulse is strong, just like she is.

"We need to get her back to the clubhouse," he informs me. I sit here, with my woman snuggled into my chest, hand petting her head and eyes closed, saying the first prayers I've said since I was a boy.

My phone begins buzzing in my pocket, but I ignore it because nothing on this earth is as important as my woman. Safe, sound, alive…that's all I can manage to comprehend at this time. It's all that matters. A year ago, I would have spit on the aspect of finding or falling in love. My childhood prevented me from seeking out those things for myself. I didn't believe in happily ever after, I didn't believe that a marriage could be good, not for me anyways.

Yet, here I am, holding the love of my life in my arms after not knowing if I'd ever see her again. Right here, right now, I realize that I'm faithfully devoted to her. My heart, my soul, it's all hers. She has the ability to make or break me, and I can't find it in me to be scared about that in the least. Because I know that they're safest with her. She treasures and covets them more fiercely than I ever did.

We don't wait long for the transport vehicle to arrive. There are two prospects driving it, good one of them can ride my bike back so I don't have to release the strong hold I've got on Lizzie. I attempt to stand up, with her still in my arms but am having a hard time getting my legs underneath me. Rip and Dust grab me under the arm pits and help me stand, I hold Lizzie close to my chest and thank them. They assist me with repositioning her so I can carefully carry her without any incidents. Once she's bridal style in my arms, her head flops to my shoulder and I quickly sprint to the vehicle. Julius has the door open and helps me get inside without hurting her any further.

No one tries to take her from me, I'd cut their throats if they even tried. Kid jumps into the front seat surprising me. "The Probees will ride our bikes home. I thought you could use someone in the driver's seat who you trust, brother." He never lets anyone ride his bike, so I'm grateful for his sacrifice for me and my Ol' lady.

"We'd all do it for each other," I'm shocked that I don't have enough wits about me to notice that I spoke my thoughts out loud.

"Thanks, brother, I appreciate it more than you'll ever know." He starts the van and puts it in drive. He's not speeding, but he's going above the posted speed limit signs we're passing.

"I know, trust me, out of all of us, I know what it's like to be in the situation you are. When Riley was missing, it was the hardest thing I've ever gone through. I remember when I got her in my arms, how unwillin' I was to let her go, and thankful more than you'll ever know that it was my mother there to drive us home. I came so close to losing her that day, a few minutes later, and she would've been on a plane and I'd never be able to find her. My brothers had my back then, and we all have yours now." I remember that day, if it hadn't been for the anonymous tip, none of us would've ever seen her again. It was a day that will forever be singed into my mind, just like today.

———

She sleeps the sleep of the dead the entire way to the clubhouse. I lovingly stroke her hair, hold her close, and whisper words of encouragement and love. I'm no poet, but I speak to her from the heart holding nothing back. I tell her more in depth about my childhood, about how I thought I'd never trust my heart to someone, how I'm so happy that she was the one who I was forced to marry...because she's the one who infiltrated my walls and boundaries.

My phone is rapidly going off in my pocket, but I can't force myself to care. I don't know who it is, or what they want, but they can go suck a big fat dick as far as I'm concerned. I'm lost in looking at my woman and admiring her when I feel the van shut off and doors open. I'm once again assisted out of the vehicle and as I pass my brothers and sisters by, I hear sniffles and cries of fear, but my only goal is to get her to our bed.

Her skin has warmed up some while we drove here. It helped that Kid noticed her blue lips and the unmistakable shiver of her body and turned the heat up. When I get her to our room, Skylar, Kassi and Kaci follow me into the room and shut the door. They help me strip her down and get her into warmer clothing.

I'd have rather had her all to myself and done these things for her, but I know her sisters needed this so I decided to not be selfish and allow them this so they'll know she's alright.

"The doc is five minutes out," Skylar tells me. I look up at her and see that her eyes are swollen, red, and there is water in them. She never cries, so my heart breaks for her, Skylar is a tough nut to crack. She doesn't show her emotions easily…unless she's pissed off at Ryder that is.

"She's okay, Sky. She's a fighter. We just need to warm her up and get some food and liquids down her." She nods her head and continues helping me get the bed turned down and I settle my woman on the mattress. The women swarm us and start tucking her in. I lay down beside her placing her head on my shoulder. I'm above the covers so it's awkward, but I manage to make it work. The ladies all kiss her on her cheek then leave us alone with longing looks as they exit our room.

"You're loved by so many, Lizzie. Don't sleep too long, okay?" I beg her, breathing in her scent that's off. She smells more of dirt, woods and pain. I didn't get her a bath, instead choosing to get her warm and ready for the doc to come take a look at her. I'll get her cleaned up after she sleeps for a few hours. I can tell she needs the rest and I don't have the heart to take that away from her. As much as I want to look into her eyes, I wanted her rested more.

As I lay here, my phone once again goes off with a notification. Finally giving in, I pull it out of my pocket and see it's a message from Andre.

Andre: got your problem all wrapped up in a pretty bow for you.

Andre: need to know where you want these assholes delivered.

Andre: Justice, answer your motherfucking phone or I'm just going to take these pretty boys' heads off.

Andre: Fine fucker, you owe me one they've been taken care of.

I can only think of one thing to reply with to his messages.

Me: Thank you

But that's only a couple of men from the Ozzie's. We still have several to hand over to the reaper of death. And I will happily serve them up on a silver platter for his delights.

Lizzie

"C'MON, BEAUTIFUL. OPEN YOUR EYES FOR ME. YOU'VE been asleep long enough, I need to hear your voice and see those beautiful chocolate brown eyes of yours." The raspy sound that comes from Justice's mouth makes me want to chastise him. I can hear that he hasn't slept in a long time. Doesn't he know he needs to take better care of himself?

I wanna cry like a toddler and stomp my feet. I don't wanna wake up, I'm nice and warm, the coziness of my cocoon has enraptured me in it's embrace. I try to move my hand to his face to push it away, only to find that I'm wrapped up in my blankets like a mummy. "Sleepy," I mutter instead. "Wake me up in an hour, I need more sleep."

"No way, baby girl. You've been asleep for two days and the animals are restless to see your smiling face."

"Two days!" I squeak out, "why on earth would you allow me to sleep for two days?" This is the first time I'm questioning his sanity.

"Cause the doc said you needed the rest. But baby, you stink, you need food and I'm tired of not being able to talk with ya."

"Well, that's rude." Who in the hell tells their wife that she stinks.

"Babe, you were in the woods for hours. Between sweating, shivering, the cold elements, the dirt, twigs, leaves and other shit that's still in your hair…let's face it, that will never sell as a perfume." What? My mind whirls as memories take over. I relive the entire nightmare all over again. No, no, nonononono! I hear a whimper escape my lips and Justice pulls me close to him. He begins murmuring in my hair, and after a few more minutes of sobs, I finally settle down.

I begin to hiccup, but know I need to apologize for being so stupid and coming up to check on him. I blurt it all out, from the minute I spotted the two boys, until the last thing I remember about spotting him and his brothers on their bikes.

"You're so smart and brave," he rumbles out.

"I'm not feeling so smart right now," I answer back.

"But you are, you never once just laid there and waited to be rescued. You came up with a plan and executed that. You got yourself to safety and found the road. You fought the pull of the darkness that wanted to take you over. You gave everything you had to make it back to me. I love you, Lizzie. I'm so damn proud of you."

My arms wrap around his neck and I bury my face in the crook of it. I sob, and sob, and sob until there's nothing left. "I love you so much, Justice. I was so scared I'd never see you again and get the opportunity to say those words…just one more time."

"I would love to hear those words escape your lips for the rest of my natural life, Lizzie."

"Then I'll make sure to say them as often as possible. Every morning that I wake, every night before I sleep and in between those times. I will remind you and show you just how much you truly mean to me."

"Thank you."

"For what?" I ask him.

"For giving me that gift. I never thought I'd have it or deserved it. But I'm so happy that I do. I'm a selfish man and I'll never let you go."

"Good, because I never want to be apart from you again."

"That's good to know, baby."

TWENTY

JUSTICE

"When are we goin' after these sons-of-bitches?" I bang my hand on the table in frustration. We're in a meeting two days after Lizzie finally awoke. The men have given me some time to spend with my woman alone and help her through her nightmares which are hit and miss. She had them while she was still out of it, but they've gotten worse since she opened her beautiful eyes.

"In two days, brother. I've been in contact with the other families and organizations and they're wanting to take them out just as much as you do, brother."

"I seriously doubt that," I rumble out.

"I promise you, Cardozo wants blood just as much as we do."

"Then where is he? I haven't seen or heard from him since she went missing!" I angrily bellow out. No one will convince me that he gives a fuck if one hair on his daughter's head has been harmed. I expected at least a phone call asking about how she is. But have I gotten one—nope, nada, not a damn thing.

"He's been making plans, he's been in contact with me and I've been advising him of her health and he paid for doc's services."

"Should I bake him a cookie in thanks?" I cross my arms over my chest. Whoop de doo, he called Kid, but not her husband? I'm still unimpressed by his lack of contact. Her mother nor sisters have even called to check in on her. What the fuck is up with this family? The Ol' ladies have barely left her side, even when I'm there taking care of her.

They brought me food, drinks, and kept my mind busy on other things. That's family, that's sisterhood, that's true devotion and loyalty at its finest.

"Sit still, shut your trap and I'll tell you what we've come up with!" he yells out, finally having enough of me running my mouth. I roll my wrist in front of me giving him the universal sign of 'please continue'. He gives me a hard, unappreciative look, but keeps going forward with the meeting. When he finishes speaking, I have to admit it's a damn good plan and I'm impressed with Cardozo's research. "We meet with the families tomorrow morning to finalize everything...two days, Justice. Then, you can take your anger out on the true enemies and we'll hopefully stop walking on egg shells around you." I should feel guilty for the way I've been acting, but the funny thing about it is, that I don't.

"Two days," I bob my head.

———

WITH TAKING CARE OF LIZZIE, PLANNING, AND MEETINGS, two days fly by. We're in our warehouse, getting guns and ammunition ready for tonight's attack. We won't be wearing our cuts, and will be going in unmarked, untraceable cars and SUVs. Each one donated to us by our very own PD and chief. They are vehicles in the impound lot that are set up for future auctions.

We have fake plates courtesy of one of our contacts. Dominique Arcola has given us some automatic weapons and launchers with all the serial numbers filed off. We've made sure to wear protective gloves to keep all prints off the weapons in case any land in the wrong hands. We aren't going in to take out just the head of the Ozzie's, we're going in with the plan of taking them all out. Even the lowest members on the totem pole.

We aren't just taking out our local problems, we have others in place and ready to take them out worldwide. We don't wanna take a chance of retaliation blowing back on our club. The Ozzie Walkers will be a forgotten gang of misfits and no one will bat an eye at their disappearance. We will be wearing masks, BDU's, and having government-issued weapons, giving off the appearance that this was sanctioned by good ole' Uncle Sam.

Our alibis have been set in place. Our women will be safe and secure. Each organization has placed their bodyguards at each individual compound to ensure that nothing happens to any of our families. Each one of us have a stake in this, and none of us want to have anything happen while we're taking out the trash.

"You ready to do this?" Riptide asks me.

"More than ready," I respond, sliding the chamber back on the gun I have in my hand. I am doublechecking each gun making sure they're loaded. I don't want any of us being caught with our pants dropped below our asses.

"Relax, brother. We've got this, we will wipe them from the planet."

"We all have to be successful," I remind them. I think that's what has me on edge. I won't be with the others, checking to see if they've managed to take out each and every member. The need to be in control of mine and

Lizzie's destiny is strangling me. I've been choking on the fear for days now. I can't even fathom the thought that things may go wrong on one of our ends.

"Suck it up, buttercup," Jackson interrupts my inner contemplations. "We've never left you with your dick swinging in the cold before and we're not fixing to start now."

"I know, but before the stakes weren't as high as they are now. This is personal, guys."

"In one way or another, it's become personal to all of us," Dust interjects.

Each one of my men has become close to my club brothers. They are even thinking about sticking around and joining the club. The brotherhood we had in the service has been missed by them and they've enjoyed the bonds they've been forming since they arrived.

A hand is placed on my shoulder. I look over and see Kid standing over me. "Everything good here?" he asks me.

"It's all good, everything is locked and loaded. We just need to put them in the vehicles and hit the road."

"All in due time, brother. We're just waiting on the other teams to arrive before we branch out and go after our targets."

"My patience is running thin," I announce.

"That's understandable, Justice. But we can't show up without all the players in tow."

"Dammit," I mutter under my breath. I'm ready to get the show on the road and draw some blood. I can't wait to see the ground littered with bodies and the crimson red splattered.

An hour later, and a lot of pacing later. Weapons are loaded and we're all in our predetermined rides. I don't pay attention to any of the conversations going on around me. I'm getting myself in the zone, ready for battle just like I have every time I've faced an enemy.

Julius is lovingly stroking his hunting knife, and I instantly know that he's in the same head space as I am. Time seems to be dragging by, until we come to a stop about a mile away from where we're infiltrating and taking out the Ozzie's. We each put on a bullet proof vest, beneath our shirts, before leaving the warehouse to guarantee our safety as much as we can.

I fill my pockets with clips and load my belt with knives, three guns and throw my rifle over my shoulder. I take my dog tags and chain that are placed on around my neck and kiss it. It's something I've done since my service days. Any time I felt like I was facing something that I could possibly not come back from, I've kissed them and said a silent well wish for my fellow brothers. Needing to feel as if I've given us as much of a chance of making it out alive and well as I could.

When we've all got our preferred weapons on our person, we begin to stealthily move through the woods. It's a good thing these guys chose to have a secluded base, we will be able to use it to our advantage. We blend in with our surroundings, Riptide, Julius, Dust, Jackson, and me are leading the group of men since we have the most experience in these types of situations.

I can feel Andre close, he never confirmed he'd be here, but I've always had this sixth sense when it comes to him. Cardozo, Arcola, Marsalis, and Jiménez's men are trailing closely behind. They each sent their most lethal and trusted soldiers to help us with this operation. It doesn't surprise me that none of them wanted to get their loafers dirty, instead depending on all of us to do the dirty work.

If it had been my daughter who'd been kidnapped and nearly died from hypothermia, I guarantee you I'd be the one leading this escapade. But no, Cardozo would rather sit back, smoke his cigar and drink his brandy before getting dirt under his fingernails.

He's a vicious man who hires others to do his bidding. He's not a man in my eyes. He's not even a true leader, because if he was, he'd be here just like Kid is. My President isn't perched on a comfy chair behind a desk, shuffling papers and passing out orders. No, he's right here beside his men.

We shuffle our way along, avoiding the snap of branches and crunching of leaves. I'm pleased to see that everyone is following our lead and doing what we are. It will make things easier and keep us out of the spotlight until we're ready to be seen and heard.

When we see lights up ahead, illuminating their space, we crouch down and stick to the shadows. We stay low, some of us duck walking and others crawling to stay unseen and unheard from the windows that are wide open. We hear what sounds like a party going on, which will allow our sounds to blend in.

My heart is racing, and my blood is pumping.

Lizzie

I'm having a hard time sitting still. I've been on the phone with my sisters for most of the day trying to preoccupy my mind. None of us know what our men are out there doing, but we have a pretty good idea. Especially once my sisters confirmed that a lot of my father's soldiers have been in and out of the house this past week. There's only a few times that this occurs, it's usually when my father is preparing for something big to take place.

I could sit here and berate myself, taking this on my shoulders as being all my fault. But Skylar put her foot up my ass—metaphorically, not literally. She was explaining to me that I didn't ask to be taken, I didn't ask to be stuck out in the woods freezing so cold that I felt it bone deep. I also know there was a reason we were asked to come here in the first place, and something deep down inside of me tells me it has something to do with this group.

I'm so used to apologizing for everything, that it didn't once occur to me that this was an issue before I came along. But my new sisters are right, I didn't ask for this, if anything I was trying to escape it before I felt the desperate need to be standing next to my Ol' man.

I'm innocent in all of this, when it hits me like a sledge hammer, I become angry. How dare those sons-of-bitches place their hands on me! How dare they take me away from the safety of my home and my family! Especially that of my man, my husband, the love of my life. The only person who's ever showed me each and every day how much I mean to him. I didn't even experience that from my own parents and someone had the gall to attempt and take that away from me!

"That's it girl, get angry," Riley encourages me.

"We should take her down to the gym and let her hit the bag a time or two," Sadie implies.

"What bag?" I come out of my reverie and asks.

"The guys keep a punching bag downstairs in the gym to help them expend some of their pent-up aggression. These men go through a lot and sometimes need something to beat up."

"I could beat something up," I agree.

"Let's go." They lead me down a set of stairs and I'm impressed by the gym. I was expecting a treadmill, weight set, and a punching bag or two. But this, this is spectacular, and I've never been so wrong about my thoughts before. There's a boxing ring in the middle and it's impressive. Off to the right are several different sets of weights and benches. Across from them are five treadmills, three ellipticals and stationary bikes.

"If I'd known this was here I'd have taken advantage of the equipment," I state in awe.

"I'm surprised Justice hasn't shown you, he's down here

every morning." I stare at her in shock, because every time I wake up he's right there beside me in bed.

"He is?"

"Four a.m. like clockwork," Skylar advises me.

"Well, that answers that question, I'm comatose at that hour."

They walk me over and show me how to properly hit the bag. They take turns holding it and punching it with me. Seems as if I'm not the only one needing to be physically doing something.

TWENTY-ONE

JUSTICE

WHEN WE CHARGE THE HOUSE, WE TAKE THEM BY surprise. They jump up and I see guns being pulled from couch cushions, boots, tucked from their backs and under different tables. It's full out pandemonium as we attack, and they defend. We are in our disguises, so they don't recognize that it's us evening the score against them. I take elation in the fact that they have no idea what they've done to collect this type of intrusion.

My focus comes back to the situation and the soldier in me comes to the forefront. I fight, pillage, destroy, and maim everyone from the other side coming into my view. I fire my gun and shoot several, my knives are buried to the hilt in others. I don't care who's getting what brand of treatment from me, my only goal is to end their miserable excuse of existence.

When the fighting comes to an end, I'm covered from head to toe in blood, the red substance coating me like a second skin. I breathe in the death that permeates in the air and finally feel a freedom from the burden falling from the weight of my shoulders.

It's over.

It's time to go home.

———

"Do we really have to leave?" Lizzie asks me with tears in her eyes. I know she's going to miss everyone here, but Templeton isn't our home and I miss my brothers something fierce.

"My job here is done, Lizzie. I need to go back home."

"Can we come back and visit soon?" I smile at her question.

"Of course, we can, beautiful. They may be a different charter, but they're still our family." She seems satisfied with my response and continues packing. We're having our things shipped back so we can take our time and enjoy the freedom of the open road. She loves riding as much as I do and all but begged me to ride the bike back.

"But, does it have to be today?" She's trying to stall us leaving, and on one hand I'm happy that she's so comfortable here, but on the other I hate that she's not looking forward to leaving with me.

"Lizzie," I say her name but nothing more.

"Fine," she breaths heavily while slamming her things around.

"It's going to work out, Lizzie. You'll see."

"If you insist, but I got a lot of go to hell looks from the women of your home club."

"Ours."

"What?" she raises her eyebrows.

"Our club," I reinforce.

"If you say so," she glumly retorts.

"Dammit, Lizzie," I sigh, not sure how to make this any easier on her and feeling as if I've failed her in some way.

"Sorry, zipping my mouth now," she says, making the zipping motion with her fingers over her mouth while clamping it shut.

"I don't want you to be sorry, baby. I just don't want to

feel like a failure when it comes to you," I embarrassedly admit.

"You could never fail me, Justice. I'm just going to miss everyone so much. I was accepted and included here. I haven't ever had that before. Forgive me," she comes up to me and pushes my shoulders to where I lose my footing and end up on the bed. She climbs on top of me and straddles my legs. "I love you, Justice. I never want you to feel like you are. If you say everything will work out, I believe and trust you when you say so. Now, give me those lips," she uses my words against me. I'm always commanding her to pucker up and lay 'em on me. I respond, giving her what she wants. "Now, let's get this done so we can put your other woman between our legs and head home." My dick just got rock hard at her words.

"I have a better idea," I insist, stripping her of her shirt.

"That's an even better plan," she says, shoving her chest forward as I play with her puckered nipples above the material of her lacy bra. It doesn't take long before we're both naked and I'm pounding away inside of her. When we both collapse from our releases, I grasp that this is what we were both in need of to get rid of our individual stress.

"Love you, beautiful," I announce.

"Love you too, my sexy biker man." I burst out in laughter, because that's the first time she's used that phrase on me, and I like it even though it's funny as fuck hearing from her.

Lizzie

THE NIGHT AFTER WE MAKE IT BACK HOME WE'RE AT THE clubhouse having a welcome home party. Ashton, the President Wasp's wife, keeps giving me dirty looks. Only this time, I don't want to back down from her harsh treatment like I did on my wedding day, so I return her dirty look.

Justice notices the exchange and gives my knee a squeeze under the table. "Trust me, it'll all work out. Give her time, baby."

I don't feel like I owe her anything, but I concede to his request and nod my head. It's a silent promise, one I'm hoping I can keep. I met Bristol, Rainey, and Kori. They are sweet and don't make me feel unwanted. I get the sentiment that they will become close friends of mine, and suddenly being here doesn't have me so glum. We drink, laugh, exchange stories of our 'alpha' men and talk about our dreams and ambitions.

I talk to Rainey and Bristol the most. I'm surprised to hear their stories—their loss is heartbreaking, and I discover that Bristol has had a worse childhood than I did. I feel an immediate connection to her, Rainey's link to her sisters and mother are phenomenal. I feel her pain when she speaks about her father and the damage his loss had on them all.

I haven't physically lost my father, but I've never felt his presence either, at least not in a positive way. Justice leads me out of the clubhouse later that evening and informs me that he had a house constructed for us while we were away. We were only gone a few short weeks, he must really have pulled some strings to get it done it that limited amount of time.

When we get to the house, he carries me over the threshold and I hold my breath at the beauty of what I'm seeing. It's like he pulled my dream home out of my head and made it a reality. The kitchen is huge! Although I don't know how to cook, I am anxious to learn.

It's open, three bedrooms and two baths. There's even an office space that he says I can use however I would like to. I have no idea what I want to do with it, but am excited to explore my options. I know I want to go to school and have a career, I just am not sure of what it is I want to do. I've never had the choice before, so I plan on taking my time and not jumping head first into something that I won't want to finish.

———

Six months later

I CAN'T KEEP MY HEAD OUT OF THE TOILET BOWL AND the taste of vomit penetrates my mouth. I must have the flu bug that's going around. I've not really ever been sick as a child, so this is the worst thing I can ever remember experiencing. It's been a week now, and I'm feeling considerably weak, and tremendously exhausted.

I fall asleep again on the bathroom floor. I've been doing this lately because the cold tile feels good against my overheated body. My body is lifted from the floor and I protest being removed from my spot. "Please, Justice. It's easier if I'm already at the toilet when my tummy rolls."

"I'll get a trash can and put it next to the bed. Doc is on his way, I'm tired of this shit, Lizzie. We need to find out what's wrong with you and treat it. I'm sick and tired of coming home to find you passed out on that damn hard floor."

"But it feels good," I implore.

"The bed will feel better," he advises me.

"According to whom?"

"Me, you deserve something soft to caress your skin, beautiful girl. I'll get a cool wrap to put around your neck while you rest." He places me down on the bed and I snuggle into my pillow top mattress and goose down feathered comforter and pillow.

"Okay," I slur when the darkness once again takes over.

I wake to the doc standing over me. He asks me questions to which I answer honestly. He takes some blood and makes me go pee in a cup. Justice is pacing the bedroom frantically while this is going on. When I go to the bathroom to do as ordered, he tries to follow me.

"I've been peeing on my own for a long time, Justice."

"You're weak, Lizzie. Let me help you."

"What are you going to do? Hold the cup under me while I try and aim?"

"If that's what I've gotta do."

"I wasn't aware you are a fan of golden showers."

"That's cause I'm not." He scrunches up his face with a disgusted look.

"Then back off, I'll call you if I need you. Okay?"

"Fine, woman. Go get this done and over with so I can get your ass back in bed."

"Yes, sir." I salute him, earning myself a look that promises retribution for my attitude.

I pee in the cup and accidentally get some on my hand because they were shaking while trying to hold it still. I hurriedly rush over to the sink and wash my hands. As I go to leave the bathroom dizziness takes hold and I have to bite my pride and call out for Justice.

"See, told ya."

"Just leave the cup in the bathroom," Doc hollers out. "I'll run my test in there," he informs us. Once I'm tucked back in he disappears behind the closed door.

"What kind of test does he need to do with your pee?"

"There's all kinds of tests they can run with your urine," I inform my man. Although I know there's one he's most likely in there running now. And if my suspicions are correct, we'll go from a family of two to a family of three sometime later this year.

Justice

MY EYES SNAP OPEN WHEN THE MOST OFFENDING SMELL IS placed under my nose. "The fuck is that?" I angrily ask looking up at doc. "And what the fuck am I doing on the floor?" I look up at my woman where she's sitting on the bed. Her face is full of mirth and I can see how hard she's holding down laughter. "What?"

"That never gets old," Doc tells her.

"What?" I say louder, getting more agitated by the minute.

"For a badass biker, you sure did pass out as soon as doc said the word pregnant," she bursts out in laughter. She's enjoying my humiliation a little too much for my liking.

"Shut it, woman."

"Make me," she states, sticking her tongue out at me.

"I see someone's feeling better," I say, looking her body over as much as I can physically see of her.

"Doc gave me something for the nausea while you were taking your short nap."

"I don't nap," I inform her.

"If you say so," she cockily exclaims. A little too cocky if you ask me. Then it slaps me in the face what she said.

"Wait a fuckin' minute, did you just announce that you're pregnant?"

"Yes," she whispers, losing her smile. I get up from the floor and walk over to her. I go down on my knees and place my hand on her stomach.

"You're having my baby?"

"Ours, I'm having our baby." Tears are running down her face. Is she scared of how I'll react?

"A baby!" I stand up whooping before I go back down on my knees. I bend over and move her hands where they are protectively placed over our growing child. I kiss it and then tell my baby, *our* baby how excited I am for him or her to be born. "You've given me everything I never knew I wanted, Lizzie. Thank you for helping me live again."

"We have learned to live again together. Thank you for all of the gifts and blessings you've given me." We end up kissing and hear the door lightly shut behind us.

This is the beginning of our forever.

Once she falls back asleep, I begin my research on what

all she can and can't do while she's pregnant. I learn what she can and can't eat, what she can and can't do physically…which shockingly isn't much. But my target research is sex, mainly can we without harming our baby. Thank God we can, because I'm not sure I can go that long without feeling her skin against mine.

As I'm lost in research my phone rings. I pick it up and look at the caller ID and see that it's Malibu.

"What's up, brother?"

"Remember when you offered to be there if I needed someone to talk to?"

"Of course, brother." My ears are picking up panic in his voice.

"I could really use that now. I'm so lost brother, I need help…"

Lizzie

WHEN I FEEL THE BED DIP, I OPEN MY EYES AND GRASP the fact that I've slept the entire day away—once again. "Everything okay?" I ask him.

"I hope so, Lizzie. I really do."

"Wanna talk about it?" Instead of answering me, he begins talking. He's worried about his friend, his brother. He tells me all about Malibu, Fern, and Kassi's relationship. Where it all began, and where it went terribly wrong with Fern's death. Malibu has just learned about how and why she truly died, and it has his head all fucked up and it's affecting his relationship with Kassi.

I can tell he loves her, anyone could with the way he used to talk about her and light up when someone mentioned her name. I am on the same page as Justice and am worried not only for his brother, but for my friend. She deserves the world and more, because she was a victim and also never felt loved or wanted by her father. It's how we bonded and became as close as we are.

"Do you think they'll get past this?" I can't help but ask.

"I don't know. I really don't and that's what worries me the most. They love each other, I would hate for them to lose sight of that fact."

"Me too."

"Now that you're awake, feel like celebrating?"

Grateful for the change of topic I emphatically nod my head. "Absolutely."

And we celebrate for the next two days. In the bedroom, in the shower, on the kitchen counters, on the washing machine and on the couch. My man is very enthusiastic with sharing his happiness and I'm more than accommodating in reciprocating his pleasure.

Life is so good.

EPILOGUE

Malibu

FOR YEARS I'VE BEEN TRYING TO SOLVE THE MYSTERY OF why Fern was murdered. I've searched high and low, spending nearly all of my life savings in an attempt to get some answers. I've hit brick wall after brick wall. No one was willing to talk to me or share what they do know.

The anonymous phone call I received earlier, floored me.

I don't understand what I learned. This wasn't the Fern I knew and loved. She told me all of her secrets, or so I thought. Did Kassi know any of this? Red hot rage takes over as I think about how she could be betraying me as much as Fern did. I'm sitting on the couch next to Kassi and can't help but look over my shoulder, wondering how much she's been keeping from me.

I love Kassi, don't get me wrong. But Fern, she was the love of my life. The one I lost and have never been able to get out of my heart. I'm not sure I'll ever get over her loss. My future was set, Kassi, Fern, and I were supposed to live happily ever after. But that was stolen from me, ripped from my arms before I knew I needed to protect it.

I can't be here, I can't look at her without wondering how deep the betrayal goes. I can't come right out and ask her about it without having a leg to stand on first.

And if she doesn't know, and I blast her with this information, it's liable to break her further than she was when she survived the attack. But she was there! She had to have heard the fight that I'm sure took place. How could she hide this from me?

"I've gotta go," I say, getting up off the couch and rushing out the door without even telling her goodbye. I need to talk to someone, someone who's not so closely involved. Someone who can look in from the outside and give me sound advice.

Kassi

When Malibu rushes out the door, my jaw hits the ground. He's never looked at me the way he just did. Fear crawls up my spine, and shivers wrack my body. Why is it I suddenly have a bad feeling that somehow, for some unknown reason to me, I've just lost him?

I've always struggled with wanting to know if he in actuality does love me, or if he settled for me after losing our third, my best friend...our Fern. Have I just been someone to warm his bed, fill a void that she left behind?

The wondering and worrying has taken its toll on me throughout the years. But I miss her so much, and love him to the depths of my soul that I was willing to overlook it to find some sort of happiness. Have I been fooling us both?

As always, with our twin ESP, my phone rings and I see it's Kaci. I glumly answer the phone.

"Hello?"

"What is it? What happened?" she frantically asks with my nephew wailing in the background.

"I don't know," I whisper, then burst out into uncontrollable sobs. "I need you."

"I'll be right there. Five minutes, sissy. Just five, stay strong until I get there."

"I'll try…"

The End

For now, until Malibu and Kassi share their story with us all in Forever Yours.

LIBERTY'S STORY

Liberty Parker

Where fantasy, romance and dreams collide.

Liberty has been an avid reader for most of her life. When she was younger she used to sit and fill spiral note-books full of stories for her grandmother. As she got older, she took the jobs needed for raising her boys as a single mom until she met her amazing husband. She has stopped working in the last few years and started off by promoting authors, then she took up blogging and reviewing for authors. This has led her down the path of writing and creating characters and telling their stories.

She loves getting creative and working behind the scenes with her characters and bringing her imagination to life.

Find me on Facebook:
https://www.facebook.com/authorlibertyparker/?
ref=bookmarks

OTHER BOOKS BY LIBERTY

Hatchet

Chief

Smokey & Bandit

Law

Capone

<u>Old Ladies Club</u>

Book 1 you can find under author Erin Osborne

Book 2 you can find under author Kayce Kyle

Book 3 you can find under Darlene Tallman

Book 4 coming soon and will be published under Liberty Parker

<u>Next Generation of RGMC</u>

Talon and Claree

Jaxson and Ralynn...TBA

<u>Nelson Brothers Trilogy</u>

Seeking Our Revenge...

Seeking My Forever...TBA

Seeking My Destiny...TBA

ABOUT THE AUTHOR

Facebook Author Page:
https://www.facebook.com/authorlibertyparker/
Liberty's Luscious Ladies:
https://www.facebook.com/groups/115379738473648
7/
Rebel Guardians Insiders:
https://www.facebook.com/groups/280929722515781/
Profile Page:
https://www.facebook.com/authorlibertypaker
Twitter: https://twitter.com/authorlparker
Newsletter sign up: http://eepurl.com/dDZGsr
Goodreads :
https://www.goodreads.com/author/show/14035441.L
iberty_Parker
Instagram: https://www.instagram.com/libertyauthor

CPSIA information can be obtained
at www.ICGtesting.com
Printed in the USA
LVHW082202180419
614769LV00024B/947/P

9 781729 164389